The croupier paused, and Cara half expected to hear a drumroll. "Mr. Kelly wins."

Mr. Kelly wins?

It took a moment for his words to sink in, and when they did Cara's head came up and her eyes locked with the man she had only hours before agreed to meet up with for a late-night assignation. His face was hard, the angles seeming to sharpen as he stared at her with retribution burning in the hot depths of his blue gaze.

His expression confused her.

He looked at her as if he knew she was a world-class stuff up. A fraud. A person who, once you scratched the shiny surface, had no worthy place in the world.

"Tell me, Miss Chatsfield. Do you deliver on that sex kitten reputation of yours, or are you something else when the glamour is stripped away?"

Aidan stood up straight and tall, lording it over those around him. His eyes narrowed and he swept the table with a contemptuous glance. "You can have your precious company, Ellery, and your contaminated money. I don't want any of it."

Ellery stared at Aidan like a broken man who still stood facing the hangman's noose. "You're letting me keep... everything."

Aidan's lip curled. "Almost." His eyes cut to Cara's, and felt pinned by his glacier-blue gaze. "Everything except her."

Step into the opulent glory of the world's most elite hotel, where the clients are the impossibly rich and exceptionally famous.

Whether you're in America, Australia, Europe or Dubai, our doors will always be open....

Welcome to

The Chatsfield

Synonymous with style, sensation...and scandal!

For years, the children of Gene Chatsfield—global hotel entrepreneur—have shocked the world's media with their exploits. But no longer! When Gene appoints a new CEO, Christos Giatrakos, to bring his children into line, little does he know what he is starting.

Christos's first command scatters the Chatsfields to the farthest reaches of their international holdings—from Las Vegas to Monte Carlo, Sydney to San Francisco.... But will they rise to the challenge set by a man who hides dark secrets in his past?

Let the games begin!

Your room has been reserved, so check in to enjoy all the passion and scandal we have to offer.

Enter your reservation number:

00106875

at

www.TheChatsfield.com

The Chatsfield

Sheikh's Scandal Lucy Monroe

Playboy's Lesson Melanie Milburne

Socialite's Gamble Michelle Conder

Billionaire's Secret Chantelle Shaw

Tycoon's Temptation Trish Morey

Rival's Challenge Abby Green

Rebel's Bargain Annie West

Heiress's Defiance Lynn Raye Harris

Eight volumes to collect—you won't want to miss out!

Michelle Conder

—

Socialite's Gamble

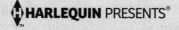
HARLEQUIN PRESENTS®

Recycling programs
for this product may
not exist in your area.

ISBN-13: 978-0-373-13255-3

SOCIALITE'S GAMBLE

First North American Publication 2014

Copyright © 2014 by Harlequin Books S.A.

Special thanks and acknowledgment are given to
Michelle Conder for her contribution to The Chatsfield series.

HARLEQUIN®
™ www.Harlequin.com

Printed in U.S.A.

All about the author...
Michelle Conder

From as far back as she can remember **MICHELLE CONDER** dreamed of being a writer. She penned the first chapter of a romance novel just out of high school, but it took much study, many (varied) jobs, one ultra-understanding husband and three very patient children before she finally sat down to turn that dream into a reality.

Michelle lives in Australia, and when she isn't busy plotting loves to read, ride horses, travel and practice yoga.

Other titles by Michelle Conder available in ebook:

DUTY AT WHAT COST?
LIVING THE CHARADE
HIS LAST CHANCE AT REDEMPTION
GIRL BEHIND THE SCANDALOUS REPUTATION

To Ris and Trish. Two great women whose generous advice and unending support buoys me up and makes me smile. Thanks for being part of my writing village! ·

CHAPTER ONE

By rights Cara should have felt like she was on top of the world.

And she had been yesterday when her agent had informed her that she had won the lucrative Demarche cosmetic contract that would take her modelling career in a more serious direction.

On some level Cara still couldn't believe her agent had pulled it off and she probably wouldn't relax until the big announcement was made at a glitzy event in London the following Sunday evening. Eight days from now.

It was going to be such a big deal that despite all her experience in the public eye, Cara knew that she would be nervous on the night. Especially when things had a tendency to go wrong for her at peak moments in her life and she had no idea why.

Not that she would let anything get in the way this time. Her agent had worked really hard to paint Cara in the best light possible. To explain that she had changed, that she was no longer the Chatsfield wild child and all-round party girl but a young woman who was revered by others around the world.

Cara secretly thought that had been pushing it a bit but Harriet Harland genuinely believed in her and Cara would not let her down. Especially after so many people had tried to distance themselves from her after that hideous rock video she had mistakenly agreed to appear in last year. Before the censorship board had pulled it, it had come with an R rating, but naturally, it had gone viral before then.

Cara had thought that she would never get a decent job again after that. Certainly that's what her father had implied.

Which brought her right back to why she couldn't yet bask in the glow of her big win.

She was late.

Seriously late.

Not entirely her fault because, really, who could have predicted that she'd get stuck on the tarmac at LAX for five hours due to an unexpected electrical storm that had hung over the city like a bad smell.

And by the look of the teeming rain outside she supposed she was lucky the plane had even landed in Vegas and not been rerouted to, say...Uzbekistan!

That would be more in keeping with the day she was having.

Probably she shouldn't have even detoured from London to LA but when she'd been told that she had to go to Vegas, she'd wanted to stop off and take her agent to lunch. Somehow lunch had turned into a private celebratory party and...well, she wouldn't waste time regretting it. No one other than her siblings had ever shown her any support in her life and Harriet had said it was important.

'More important than tonight,' she grumbled, wanting to kiss the aisle as the line of passengers started to shuffle towards the exit doors.

Poker was hardly noteworthy even if the game she was supposed to hostess later that night at one of her father's flagship hotels had the largest buy-in of any casino in the western world. It was only a game.

Glancing at the time on her phone she shoved it back into her shoulder bag and strode down the aerobridge.

One hour.

One hour that apparently included a thirty-minute taxi ride from McCarran International to the glittering diamond on the Las Vegas strip—the Chatsfield International.

It had once had the reputation as the best casino in Las Vegas. Her father's recent appointment of the new CEO—the gorgeous but arrogant Christos Giatrakos—was an attempt to re-establish that. In fact, Christos had been given the task of revamping all the Chatsfield Hotels and thereby restore the family name to its former glory.

Former before her mother had walked out on them all years ago and her father had found the bottle and his next mistress. Now he'd met yet another woman and—surprise, surprise—he had found a new lease on life.

Christos, who took his job far too seriously in Cara's mind, had deemed that all her siblings had to be involved. Something all of them had resented as much as she did!

Rightly, or wrongly, the family business interested her about as much as moving into a nuclear-waste facility.

And she wasn't above admitting, at least to herself, that it had hurt when Christos had emailed to 'inform' her that he was sending her to Vegas to hostess some important high-rollers' poker game—supposedly the hottest ticket on the Chatsfield's gambling calendar—because deep down she knew that he was just trying to get her out of the way so that her siblings could get on with the more serious tasks.

Cara would have liked to have told him to go to hell when he had suggested it but beneath the implicit threat that she'd be cut off from her inheritance, just like her siblings, something had stopped her. There had been a tone to his words that implied that she *couldn't* do it. That the 'wild child' wasn't as good as her older siblings. It had raised her hackles and made her want to show him. And her father. Not that her father would say anything if she did a good job. He probably wouldn't even notice.

No doubt cutting her hair into a cute pageboy bob and dying it pink hadn't been the smartest thing to do though, and she wondered if her sister, Lucilla, wasn't right that she'd done it to get back at Christos and his derogatory 'It's time you did something worthwhile for the family name, Cara. After all, it paid for your fancy education when you were growing up and provided you with everything your heart desired.'

Cara had really hated him in that moment and had wanted to inform him that actually it hadn't given her everything her heart had desired. It hadn't given her two parents who loved her.

But Cara would show him tonight. And next week when the announcement was made about her new modelling contract her father would have to finally acknowledge that not only did she exist, but that she was a force to be reckoned with, as well!

Feeling more empowered she strode into McCarran International with purpose, the bright lights and the sounds of the poker machines in action greeting her, along with the smell of air freshener and polish.

Welcome to Vegas, she thought somewhat grudgingly. Her normal world was far behind her and she felt a bit like Dorothy in Oz, who would give anything to return to her normal existence. She almost glanced around her seeking out the wicked witch but she knew the evil warlords in her life were back in London, miles away. Thank heavens.

She wheeled her Vuitton overnight case behind her and strode through the throng of commuters, ignoring curious eyes that happened to fall her way. Thanks to her name, her modelling career and her tendency to cause a scandal even when she didn't mean to, her face was well-known.

She sighed. Yes, her life was a goldfish bowl; it always had been, so why was that bothering her lately when before she hadn't given a toss?

Taking a deep breath to ease the sudden constriction in her throat she told herself that everything would be fine. She was here. And an hour—okay, fifty minutes—was time enough to get to the hotel, shower, dress and brief herself on who would be seated at her father's esteemed poker table. Something she would already know if the casino hadn't sent her a corrupted file she'd been unable to open on the plane.

Whatever.

She was good at thinking on her feet. She just had to get her feet and the rest of herself to the hotel. And fast. Tonight was just one of those nights that had to be endured.

No, she corrected herself, not endured so much as *conquered*.

She gave a faint smile as she took in her skinny arms and legs, her delicate high-heeled gladiator sandals. She wasn't exactly 'conqueror' material. She never had been.

But still, she wouldn't muck up tonight. Her pride demanded that she didn't.

Hearing her phone ring, and glad for the divergence, Cara sidestepped a group of tourists and didn't break stride as she reached into her bag to retrieve it.

Fumbling she glanced down and only just got the impression of a tall, well-dressed man in a hurry, his long legs eating up the space between them, a dark scowl on his square jaw as she sidestepped again and he ran right into her.

He didn't make a sound but Cara gasped at the impact, her foot twisting alarmingly beneath her. She would have toppled right into him but his reflexes were lightning fast and he gripped her upper arms and held her upright. His hold was hard and firm and she felt the jolt of his touch almost as if she'd had an electric current pass right through her.

Shocked, she stared up at him and for a moment she forgot to breathe. Rich blue eyes stared—no, glared—back at her in a beautifully boned face that could only be described as hard. Angular.

In the blink of an eye she took in his short, dirty-blond hair, straight nose and a firm surly-looking mouth ringed by what looked like a day's beard growth. It was a beautiful, masculine face that brought to mind a warrior battling it out on the Scottish highlands with nothing but a shield and a powerful sword.

A powerful sword?

Slightly flustered by her startling reaction to a stranger, Cara frowned. 'Can you please watch where you're going next time?'

'Can I...?' Aidan Kelly narrowed his eyes between thick lashes and stared at the woman in front of him. He'd just been in transit for thirty-three ungodly hours from Australia to get here and he was tired, hungry, aggravated and in a hurry, and this pink-haired waif had the audacity to accuse him of being in the wrong. 'Lady, I *was* watching where I was going. You were the one with your head stuck in your bag.'

'I stepped out of your way and—oh, no!' She glanced down between them. 'I think you broke my shoe.'

Aidan made a disgusted noise. 'I haven't broken anything.'

Twisting her foot out to the side she ran her hand down her long, slender legs and Aidan's eyes couldn't help but follow her movements. He felt an unexpected stirring of lust in his blood and his frown deepened. Had she just done that deliberately to get his attention?

'Damn,' she muttered softly. 'It *is* broken.'

Aidan rolled his eyes. Not his problem. 'Next time you might want to look where you're going.'

She stared at him open-mouthed as if she couldn't believe him and that made two of them because he couldn't quite believe her, either.

'And next time you might remember this is not a race-track,' she said prissily, moving her foot gingerly inside her sandals that hugged her slender calves all the way up to her knees. 'These are my favourite shoes,' she grouched at him. 'I've had them for years.'

He cast them a disparaging glance. 'Fascinating. Now excuse me, I need to be somewhere.'

She shook her head as if he completely disgusted her and hobbled over to a nearby seat, the words *rude* and *irresponsible* and *typical male* ringing in his ears.

Aidan's back straightened. If there was one thing he was, it was responsible, and there was no way this pompous English totty was going to pin the blame for her broken shoe on him.

'What did you just say?' His voice was low, the softness of it underlying a lethal menace she would do well to heed in his current frame of mind.

He had important business to take care of at the Chatsfield Casino and every minute he spent with her was a minute he wasn't focused on his end goal.

Her lower lip trembled as he towered over her and he planted his hands on his hips. 'And here comes the waterworks,' he scorned.

She stared at him and he had a moment of wondering

where he had seen her face before. Then he discarded the thought. He didn't know her and he didn't want to know her.

'You are really not a nice man, are you?'

He shook his head as if to say *lame, very lame* and reached into his pocket to withdraw his wallet. 'Here's a fifty.' He held the money out to her. 'That should cover it.'

She looked at his offering as if he'd just pulled it off the bottom of his shoe. 'Hardly.' She lifted her chin and her hair fell back from her face. She was really quite exquisite with her chin jutting out like that. Her lips a strawberry pink, her cheekbones high and her eyes heavily lashed. With mascara, no doubt.

'These shoes are worth a thousand pounds.'

Aidan blinked, realising that he'd lost his train of thought while he'd been staring at her. Pulling himself together he raked her slender frame and let an insolent curl shape his mouth. 'I doubt it, honey.'

'Honey?'

'Look, lady, I get it. Run into someone and then try to fleece them. Sorry, I'm not that gullible.'

'Fleece them?'

If possible her eyes widened even more and he refused to let himself be drawn in by her. Refused to glance down at the sexy thrust of her small breasts or those long silken legs showcased to perfection in tiny denim shorts. 'Look, I don't know if you're a broke tourist on the make or a working girl but I don't like being played for a fool.'

'A working…' Her eyes narrowed and he felt pinpricks of heat on his skin as she dragged her eyes down over his lightweight suit and then back up. He saw her shoulders straighten and noticed that a hot flush had risen up along her amazing cheekbones.

Then she rose in front of him like Cleopatra on the throne and for a minute he expected to feel the sharp sting of her small hand connecting with his face. Lucky for her she pulled herself back in time and only stuck her nose up at him.

'You really are a horrible man.'

Aidan shook his head. He didn't have time for her games. 'For all I know the shoe was already broken,' he said curtly.

'For all you *care*, you mean,' she spat at him. 'I hope you have an interesting life,' she said, smiling coldly before grabbing hold of the handle of her suitcase.

If he wasn't mistaken, Aidan thought, the little witch had just blessed him with a Chinese curse.

About to give her a true piece of his mind and tell her just what he thought of her benign attempts to extort money out of him, he heard his name being decimated by a shrill female voice.

'Mr Kelly? Oh, Mr Kellllly?'

Aidan turned to find the stewardess who had dogged his every move during the flight from hell bearing down on him like a Hungarian linebacker. 'Oh, Mr Kelly. I'm so glad I found you.' She flashed all her teeth at him like a barracuda spying lunch. 'I have something for you.'

He just had time to see the pink-haired woman roll her eyes heavenward before disappearing into the crowd. Frustrated that he hadn't had time to deal with her impertinence properly, he glared at the stewardess in front of him. 'This had better be good.'

As soon as the out-of-breath stewardess had placed her manicured hand against her chest in a move redolent of Scarlett O'Hara, her posture giving the impression that she'd like nothing better than to plaster herself all over the front of the man Cara had nicknamed 'the cretin jerk,' she knew it was her cue to disappear. No doubt it was her phone number that she wanted to give him. Or maybe she was about to drag him off to the nearest broom cupboard and put those pearly whites to good use. Cara didn't care, but she hoped he picked up a nasty disease in the process.

Rude, horrible, *loathsome* man!

Fuelled by angry frustration and nervous energy at the disappearing time, Cara did what she did best—she retreated from the situation and merged with the noise and bustle of those around her as she hobbled towards the terminal exit with as much dignity as she could muster, thankful that she would never have to see that man's arrogant face again.

The airport was teeming with people and outside it was raining so hard she was sure it was a monsoon. How was it possible to be raining in LA *and* Vegas? Wasn't California supposed to be always sunny? And Sin City was in the middle of the desert. It should be hot, she thought as she stepped through the automatic glass doors and into an icy cold wind that sawed the breath from her lungs. Holy moly, but tonight could freeze the ice off a penguin.

Rubbing her hands over her arms and trying to stop her knees from knocking together with cold she quickly scanned the long line of bedraggled commuters—also underdressed to withstand the arctic blast, and the non-existent taxis that should have been lining the kerb. Why was it that taxi cabs seemed to disappear in every country unused to inclement weather? She'd do anything for the reliability of the black cabs back home right now because she couldn't be late. She just couldn't.

Quelling another bout of panic she gritted her teeth and marched back inside, searching for the hire-car desks.

She stopped when she saw them. It seemed a couple of hundred other commuters had already had the same idea. Frustrated she headed back outside and saw the line surge forward as three taxis pulled alongside the kerb and just as swiftly departed with relieved customers inside.

A shiny silver limousine purred up to the sidewalk, water drops clinging to its polished windows and paintwork like tiny pearls and the crowd gazed at it longingly. Oh, what she'd give to have thought ahead and organised one of those. She watched the young driver alight from the car and scan the crowd. Glancing around, she waited to see who had won the lottery and then back at the chauffeur when no one came forward. He had a sign and Cara shifted a little to the right so she could read it.

Mr Kelly, it read in bold print.

'Mr Kelly? Oh, Mr Kelllly?' The stewardess's high-pitched voice filled Cara's head and she narrowed her gaze. Surely not. Could Mr Kelly be the cretin jerk from inside? And why did his name sound so familiar?

Not that she was truly interested. He was probably just an overinflated film star and the outrageous idea of taking off in his plush Mercedes jumped from outer space and straight into her mind. His *warm*, plush Mercedes.

Of course she wouldn't do it, but boy, she'd like to. It would serve him right for his scathing put-down of her before.

Cara looked back through the terminal, half expecting him to swagger towards her with the 'me Jane you Tarzan' stewardess. Really, he didn't deserve that car. Another gust of wind whipped an ice cap off the Arctic Circle and settled it over Vegas.

Even her bones shivered this time.

A nearby child sneezed and started whimpering.

'It's not supposed to rain in Vegas,' a middle-aged woman with two young children huddled under her arms groused good-naturedly.

'It's not supposed to be cold, either,' Cara said.

'Oh, my, you're Cara Chatsfield, aren't you?'

'Guilty.' Cara smiled, expecting that the woman would either turn away now in disgust, or bubble over with excitement at having met her.

'Oh, you poor thing,' she gushed. 'I'm sorry to say I read about that awful scandal last year and I just want you to know that you were right to sack that manager of yours.'

It had been her agent that she'd sacked but Cara was so shocked by the woman's passionate support she was almost stupefied. 'Well, thank you.'

'I think it's awful how people take advantage of others. And you copping all the flak for that video because you're a woman. I noticed that man in it with you wasn't mentioned and he wasn't wearing much more than you.'

'No.'

'Sorry, I'm ranting.' The woman blushed and fussed over one of the children's hair.

'No, please.' Cara smiled. 'Rant away.'

The woman grinned back. 'I wish that limousine was waiting for me. Who do you suppose it's here for? A prince?'

Cara arched a brow. 'Hardly.'

She looked around. Maybe the cretin jerk really had visited that broom cupboard.

She smiled at the woman as the idea of stealing *Mr Kellllly's* limo returned. 'Maybe it is waiting for us.'

'I wish,' the woman said with a sigh.

When one of the younger of the children started sneezing Cara straightened her spine and strolled towards the young limousine driver. 'Sorry to keep you waiting,' she said airily. 'I spotted an old friend.'

'Ma'am?'

'You are waiting for me, aren't you?'

'Ah, no, ma'am. I'm waiting for a Mr Kelly.'

Cara tilted her head and gave him a smile she'd been told made grown men forget their own names. 'It was supposed to be *Ms* Kelly, but never mind. No harm done.'

'And you're…Ms Kelly?'

'No, I'm not.' Cara smiled patiently. 'I'm travelling incognito. I have to do that after, well, you know…the video clip last year.'

The young driver blushed as Cara had expected he would and looked flustered. 'Oh, I don't—'

She waved her hand dismissively. 'Please, I'd rather not talk about it. Now, I hope you don't mind but I promised to give my friends a lift. It's too cold for them to wait for a taxi.'

'No, no.' He scampered to open the passenger door for her. 'Not at all, Miss Chats—I mean, Ms Kelly.'

Feeling just the teensiest bit guilty and determined to ignore it, Cara beckoned to the woman and her children. 'It seems the limo was waiting for me after all. Would you like a lift?'

'Oh, wow. Really?'

'Of course, but…we should hurry.'

The guilty feeling persisted for quite a way to the hotel and probably if she could relive that moment she might act differently, but it was too late now and her awed passengers had been so relieved and grateful it had been worth it.

Thankfully she'd never have to see Mr Kelly again, but maybe she'd try and find out where he was staying and send him an anonymous bottle of champagne to thank him for the ride.

She stifled an impish grin at the thought. He was really going to be livid when he realised that his car had been commandeered by someone else. In a way, she almost wished she was able to see his face.

She hoped it turned purple.

CHAPTER TWO

AIDAN SAW A flash of pink hair and one long slim leg before the limousine pulled away from the kerb, its tail-lights blinking in the gloomy night.

Amazing. The woman he had thought a cheap tourist at best could afford a limousine. Or perhaps she'd had a rich lover waiting outside.

With legs like hers it was probably the more likely scenario. Long and golden brown. He had no doubt they'd be smooth to the touch and his hand would have no trouble sliding all the way up to those tiny shorts. He imagined her breathless little gasp as he slid one finger inside the leg of those shorts and teased— What the…?

He pulled himself up short as he realised he was turning himself on.

Rubbing at the space between his eyes he shook his head. He must be going mad to fantasise about a woman like that.

A woman who wore clothes that revealed more than they hid. Well, okay, her purple blouse had been loose and only hinted at the small, high breasts beneath, but it had been designed to make a man think about exactly what they would look like underneath. And those shoes? If they hadn't been created with sex in mind, he didn't know what was.

Oh, she had been advertising, all right, and although his body had perked up with interest at her wares he'd had no intention of taking the bait. He was in Vegas for one night and one purpose and it had nothing to do with bedding a woman.

He buttoned his jacket against the cold and glanced around for his limousine. His HR manager had assured him that it would be waiting at the kerb as soon as he exited the main terminal and he was a man who knew how to do his job.

Noticing a white sign on the damp pavement he walked closer and saw that it had his name printed on it.

His gaze narrowed. Why would a piece of cardboard with— Son of a… She'd stolen his limousine!

Aidan stared at the section of road the large car had long disappeared down and knew his mouth was hanging open.

He pulled out his phone and started scrolling through his emails to get to the one that would hold the information about which car company his HR manager had used. Unfortunately he already had over one hundred new emails and he didn't have the patience to find it.

Gritting his teeth and silently imagining every way he could slowly dismember the lanky pink-haired waif he would hunt down as soon as he'd completed his business in Vegas, he raised his eyes to the darkening sky.

There were too many grey clouds for him to locate the moon but he was sure if he could it would be full. Usually, he wasn't a superstitious person but how else to explain a day that had started out great and gone downhill at a rate of knots. First his PA had quit, claiming he was too hard a taskmaster. Then his trip to Sydney airport had been plagued by an impromptu demonstration against the live export of animals—a worthy cause he might have contributed coin to had they not held him up for so long—only to arrive at the airport to find his plane had mechanical issues and had been grounded. The only available flight out of Sydney for Vegas had one seat available.

And it hadn't been first class.

Not that he was a snob. Far from it. He'd grown up in a low- to middle-class home and didn't start travelling first class until he had turned his father's business around in his early twenties.

No, it wasn't coach per se that had bothered him but being squashed into a seat his tall frame didn't easily accommodate and trying to work during what should have been a sixteen-hour flight while others slept or watched movies. Then there had been the small child who kept poking its fingers through the back of the seat and dislodging his paperwork on the tiny tray they called a table.

He sighed wearily. His currently dishevelled state wasn't exactly the way he had planned to greet his nemesis, Martin Ellery, but okay, he'd make it work. A part of him had been considering some sort of revenge against this man for fourteen years and it had become all-consuming twelve months ago when his father had passed away.

Tonight it would happen, and no matter how many obstacles got in his way Aidan wouldn't countenance failure. Had, in fact, never failed at anything in his life. And he couldn't fail at this because he had promised his father on his deathbed that he would get back at the man who had ruined his life. And a promise was a promise. Something meant to be honoured.

Unfortunately the Chatsfield casino house rules were very specific on this night that would pit some of the best and wealthiest gamblers against one another. If you missed the start of play you couldn't join the game.

He checked his watch and his agitation grew.

Just when he was contemplating the possibility of hiring a helicopter a cavalcade of taxis came into view and the line of weary commuters cheered.

A crumpled but chic businesswoman paused before getting into the first cab. She looked at him.

Aidan had seen that look on women's faces plenty of times before and he'd already noticed this one eyeing him off for the past five minutes.

'Would you like to share?' she asked.

The offer was for more than a taxicab and they both knew it. But he could allay her of that expectation on the way into town.

'Sure.'

Thirty-nine minutes later Aidan was clean-shaven, dressed in a black suit and black dress shirt—no tie because he hated them—and paused in the doorway to the Chatsfield Hotel's prestigious Mahogany Room.

It was opulent, but he already knew that. Large crystal chandeliers sparkled off polished mahogany wood panelling and a curved bar with fancy velvet stools lined the far wall. The room was already half full and scented with the faint traces of Cuban cigar smoke and the sweet scent of too many perfumes mixed together. It wasn't his usual world, but looking at him now—carelessly poised for action—no one would guess he was about to destroy another man's livelihood.

Ice clinked in a glass and Aidan surveyed the elegant crowd. A few of the men he would play against were already seated at the main table. Martin Ellery wasn't one of them. Aidan glanced around the room. Where was the slimy bastard anyway?

And then he saw him and his heart skipped a beat.

Because he wasn't alone. He was standing to the side of the bar with none other than the pink-haired waif who had stolen his limousine!

Aidan's eyes swept over her. She looked surprisingly classy in a fitted black dress that skimmed her light curves to midthigh. She had on stockings—or would they be those high-topped ones that clung to her thighs and didn't require a garter belt—what were they called? Stay-ups?—and another pair of skyscraper heels. It took his brain about point four seconds to jump to him seated on a king-size bed with her standing before him in just those stockings and heels.

Damn.

To his mind there was only one reason a woman was in the high-rollers' room of a casino. She was either looking to pick up a rich man, or she already had. That might be a gross generalisation he was sure the women's libbers would want to slice him in half for but he didn't care.

He had been a wealthy man for long enough to know the score. And this woman—*this car thief*—was on the make, any moron could see that.

He recalled the uppity curse she had delivered at the airport as sweetly as if she had been blessing his firstborn child. He nearly smiled. Then Ellery leaned closer to her.

Had Ellery already laid claim to her?

It wouldn't surprise him. His last wife hadn't been dead eighteen months but even before she'd died it had been rumoured he'd moved on. *Loyalty* was not a word Martin Ellery knew the meaning of, or cared about.

His and Ellery's paths hadn't crossed for about that long and Aidan doubted they'd have much to say to each other tonight. Ellery would know better than to try. He knew Aidan loathed him.

And for some reason he loathed the way the older man kept stroking the back of his car thief's hand in a brief caress that told any other male watching that she was unavailable.

A sick feeling rose up in his stomach. No doubt if she

was with Ellery he'd brought her to the game for good luck. Unfortunately it would take more than a statuesque model type to bring him luck tonight.

His car thief stepped back and gave Ellery a flirtatious smile and Aidan was once again caught off guard by a powerful bolt of sexual awareness so hot it burned through his bloodstream. Watching her closely, he couldn't figure out what exactly it was about her that drew him so intensely and he was mildly irritated by his reaction. Yes, she had a certain feline grace about her. A certain leggy beauty, but the girl had run off with his hire car and only a woman with no morals, or an over-exaggerated sense of entitlement, would do something like that.

Neither type appealed to him.

'Can I get you a drink, sir?'

Aidan turned his head as a waitress stopped beside him.

'No. I'm here to play poker.' He noticed that Ellery had moved to the main table and the pink-haired car thief with the kissable mouth was now alone.

He wondered what she'd do when she spotted him.

Fortunately he didn't have to wait long to find out. As if sensing his perusal she glanced up and around. He counted to six before her gaze collided with his. Keeping his expression intentionally bland he watched her eyes widen like Bambi facing down a pack of hungry mountain lions.

Oh, God!

He'd followed her.

Cara couldn't believe it. And he'd gotten into the Mahogany Room which was invitation-only. Her heart raced at the sight of him. Did he know what she had done? That she had borrowed his car? But of course he must. Why else would he be here?

Everyone else in the room seemed to fade away as he

continued to stare at her and Cara was aware of nothing beyond the beating of her own heart. And his eyes.

Standing just inside the doorway he was at once invisible and totally conspicuous. His aura alone dominated the busy room. Which shouldn't have been possible in a place full of the rich and famous. Still, he did and she wasn't the only woman who had noticed him. She could tell by the low murmur of appreciation by the women on her right that he was being favourably sized up as a potential catch.

And Cara had to get rid of him. Quickly, before the big game started and before he caused a scene that would get back to Christos.

Deciding that the best course of action was the direct one, she tried to still the jittery feeling in her legs and walked towards him.

The room felt like it had just tripled in length and she fervently hoped that he didn't know that she had been the one who had taken his car.

Would the hire-car company have told him already?

Blast her impulsive decision to colour her hair so brightly. For once she'd be happy to be her normal boring self because a girl with muddy-brown hair would have been so much harder to locate.

But what if he wasn't looking for her about the car? What if he still thought she was a working girl he'd decided to purchase for the night? A buzz went through her body at the possibility and she was horrified to find that despite everything she was actually totally attracted to him.

At some point she hoped that she would be able to laugh at the day she'd just had. Some point in the very distant future. Right now, though, she would forget all about her unhelpful hormones and the way his eyes shone like brilliant sapphires against his olive skin and black shirt.

Of course she felt sick the closer she came, her stomach clenching and unclenching like a giant-size fist, and when his gaze swept over her body her confidence completely deserted her.

She stopped directly in front of him but with enough room between them to fit at least two buses. 'I'm sorry,' she began a little breathlessly, 'but this room is invitation only.'

His level gaze raked her face and then he smiled. 'Ah, the woman whose shoe I broke.'

Cara's heart skipped a beat at the sound of his rich, deep voice. 'Well, you didn't break it exactly.' She let out a nervous laugh. 'It was an accident. And you were right. I should have been paying more attention to where I was going.'

'Generous of you considering it was I who ran into you,' he said pleasantly. Too pleasantly.

He knows about the car, she thought a little desperately, her eyes searching his. She felt it with every guilty bone in her body.

Hoping her face wasn't flushed even though she felt like it was pressed against a heating pad she told herself to calm down. Maybe he didn't know. Maybe it was her own sense of guilt making her feel paranoid. 'Please, don't mention it again.' She cleared her throat. 'Now, I'm sorry but I'm going to have to ask you to—'

She stopped speaking and stared up at his bemused expression.

Mr Kelly. Mr Kellllly.

Aidan Kelly?

Like one of the poker machines downstairs that had just hit the jackpot Cara's brain lit up with where she had seen this man's face before. Unfortunately he wasn't some matinee idol; he was *the* Aidan Kelly of KMG—Kelly Media Group. The founder of some huge network TV station in

Australia that had expanded to dominate the US entertainment industry and recently had something to do with British TV, as well. She couldn't remember what, but she did remember he was as rich as they came and his influence was global. He was also rude and full of himself but... She swallowed heavily. 'You have an invitation.' Her voice came out as little more than a squeak and his smile grew.

'Why else would I be here?' he asked softly.

No reason, Cara thought wildly, *no reason at all*. No reason other than to play poker at *her* table.

She groaned inwardly. The night was ruined. She was dead. He would complain to Christos and then... She had to apologise. Had to admit to her desperate actions at the airport. Admit how late she had been, how desperate, how—

No, she wouldn't let herself panic and ruin everything. Because what if he didn't know and she admitted her mistake and made everything ten times worse. No, she would do what her brother Franco had taught her to do in situations like this and play the dead bat—an old cricketing term. Franco would be impressed that she had even remembered.

As plans went it wasn't the greatest, but it would have to do until she came up with something better.

'Well then, Mr...'

She let the silence fill between them as she waited for him to provide his name. His mouth kicked up at one corner. 'Kelly. Aidan Kelly.'

Bond, James Bond had nothing on this man, she thought helplessly.

'Well, I apologise for the misunderstanding, Mr Kelly, and am pleased to welcome you to the Mahogany Room. My name is Cara Chatsfield and—'

'I thought I recognised you. Apart from the shoes, of course.'

Cara smiled and her lips felt like they were about to crack. 'Yes, well. As I was saying, I'm the hostess for the game this evening so if you would like to follow me we'll get underway.'

He fell into step beside her and Cara slowly released a pent-up breath. Maybe, just maybe, she was going to get away with this.

'I apologise for being late,' he said easily. 'I was…' Cara glanced up at him when he hesitated. His smile widened and her pulse raced. 'Delayed at the airport.'

Oh, God. 'Nothing drastic, I hope?' she said a little too breathlessly.

'No.' He shrugged. 'Nothing I can't handle, at least.' His smile turned lupine and Cara felt dizzy.

She knew her actions in taking his hire car were far from admirable and there was no use pretending she had done it because of a couple of small children. Yes, she had loved being able to get them in out of the cold, but really she'd been beyond desperate and she'd been smarting from his condescending attitude towards her.

The need to admit to what she had done made her stomach feel like it was full of battery acid, but something held her back.

She did plan to apologise. To explain that she had been stressed, upset…a little put off by his gruff manner. None of that was an excuse but…it had happened and she would deal with it. She would pull herself out of yet another mess of her own making. The big question was, when would she learn to stop reacting when someone formed a low opinion of her?

Tomorrow.

Tomorrow she would go to him and apologise. After tonight was over.

'Yes, it was terribly busy, wasn't it?' she said briskly.

Having made her mind up to put off the inevitable, the only option left open to her was to keep pretending that everything was completely as it should be.

Feeling marginally better when he didn't make another comment, she showed him to his seat on the raised circular dais that held the main table and plastered a serene smile on her face. When he handed her his jacket she reached for it, only to find it suspended between both their hands. The wonderful scent of spice and earthy man rose between them and when he didn't immediately release the jacket she glanced up. His face was closer than she expected, his blue eyes deep pools of lethal sensuality. The heating pad that had attached itself to her face increased a few more degrees until her cheeks stung with it.

'Oh, and, Miss Chatsfield?'

She blinked, unable to do anything but stare. 'If you wouldn't mind getting the phone number of the local police for me. I have an incident to report and I didn't have time to do it before.'

Oh, God. This was it. She would once again be confirmed as the airheaded younger sister of the Chatsfield family. The naughty girl. The one who shouldn't have even been there.

And she had no one else to blame but herself.

'Incident?' she said weakly, wondering if she threw herself at him and begged for mercy if he would listen. Then she remembered his icy disdain and arrogance at the airport.

'Nothing for you to worry about,' he said, finally letting go of the jacket to take his seat.

CHAPTER THREE

AIDAN LEANED BACK in the velvet-lined chair at the main gaming table and hooked his arm over the back.

The suspense must be killing her, he thought, shocked to find that he was enjoying himself. He'd almost whistled a merry tune when she'd nearly fainted dead away in front of him after he'd mentioned the police.

He had no intention of calling them, of course, but feeling her worried eyes on him all evening would be punishment enough.

Or would have been if those tingling little glances didn't have the unexpected result of making him totally aware of her, as well.

It was unconscionable, really, to have his attention so divided when he needed to focus the most.

But okay, so far, the game was going according to plan. Ellery was anxious enough to make some rash plays, but not enough to make him quit. Aidan knew the old bastard loved nothing more than to look good in front of his compatriots and would want to finish the game on a high.

Aidan's clear-eyed gaze fell on him now, the older man's attention once again firmly wedged somewhere in the vicinity of Cara Chatsfield's cleavage.

He told himself he was glad Ellery had been as distracted by her as many of the other men at the table because it made his job that much easier.

Still, he felt his jaw knot as he watched her smile and work the table, her long-limbed sensuality and graceful movements promising hours of untold delights.

She was very practiced for one so young. And very comfortable having older men paw her. Or was she? Now and then Aidan was sure he'd caught a hint of uncertainty in her expression. A hint that she wasn't enjoying herself half as much as she pretended.

Yeah, he mocked himself, *she's a real woman of substance*.

She played them. Some knew it and played along, hoping to get her into the sack anyway, but some didn't and they were all but salivating. Aidan wondered if she was just biding her time. Waiting to see which one of them ended up on top before making her move. It would match his experience of women.

So why then, he asked himself not for the first time, did he find her so damned attractive?

An oil-rich sheikh broke into his unwanted musings by calling a time-out to use the bathroom. The croupier gave them fifteen minutes and all the men got up to stretch. Aidan didn't. He could sit here all night if it meant destroying Martin Ellery. And he was more than halfway there.

His prowess, he knew, had surprised Ellery because Aidan wasn't by nature a gambler. He'd always been too conservative. Like his father. But he knew poker was Ellery's weakness and so Aidan had painstakingly learned the game. Learned to be good at it. His natural tendency to hide his emotions helped. Another trait he shared with his father.

His now-*dead* father, thanks to Martin Ellery's criminal machinations fourteen years ago that had broken his father's spirit. And now Aidan would break his. He would snap it in half. He would systematically destroy his pride, his reputation, his confidence… Hell, he wanted Ellery to lose his very reason for living. No man deserved it more.

And Ellery knew he was on the ropes; his dwindling stack of chips signified his run of rash calls and bad bluffs was coming to an end. A smarter man would have got up and walked away by now. Ellery's ego would keep him at the table. Aidan knew it and he counted on it.

Stretching his legs out in front of him he signalled for another glass of iced tea. He hated the stuff, but to the other players it looked like whisky and it put them at ease. Made him look like a serious player.

Absently he noticed that Ellery had crossed the room and was holding Cara Chatsfield's arm and once again, his gut tightened. The man had been pawing her all night and by the sound of Cara's husky laugh she didn't mind.

So hell, why should he?

It wasn't like she was some naive little nobody. This was a woman who would go to the opening of an envelope. And for sure he had been wrong about the hint of vulnerability he'd noticed earlier. Maybe he'd been seeing something he wanted to see in her.

And why, he asked himself, would he want this woman to be anything other than what she was?

A vacuous bimbo. He let his eyes wander up her creamy throat to her full mouth and slanted emerald-green eyes ringed with black kohl. They had to be as fake as her hair. Though as to the latter he would admit that the pink gamin hairdo made her look like an erotic pixie. A very tall erotic pixie.

Just then she leaned closer to Ellery to hear whatever dribble was coming out of the swine's mouth and he hated the dazzling smile on her face as she led him from the room. It was open and engaging and transformed her from beautiful to the kind of woman men went to war over.

And where the hell were they going now? Ellery's suite? The break was only fifteen minutes. Surely Ellery would want to savour her if he got that chance.

Annoyed with the direction of his thoughts, Aidan settled more deeply into his chair and absently watched the glittering crowd. There were only two ways to make it into this room. Money or promise. The men usually had the former, the women the latter. It was the lay of the land. But not usually his land. Aidan usually worked, worked out and slept. In that order. Occasionally he dated and even more occasionally he joined members of his executive team for a drink. But since the death of his father last year, he'd been driven by a deep, yearning restlessness. A restlessness that he would finally put to bed after he crushed Martin Ellery and took everything that he held dear—his company and his self-worth.

Frowning as his gaze lingered on the private doorway Ellery and Cara had disappeared through, he tried to tell himself that the Chatsfield socialite was not his problem. That it was not his job to protect her if she was too stupid to see the man for what he was.

Aidan had made it a point years ago never to become emotionally involved in any issue, and really, Cara Chatsfield did not seem like the kind of woman who needed protecting from anyone but herself.

So did he care about whether or not the old man had his hands inside her dress? If he had his mouth on hers? If he was kissing his way down her creamy throat—

Hell.

'Where does that door lead?' he snarled.

The startled waitress he'd just accosted stared up at him.

'The High Stakes bar and balcony that overlooks the Strip. But both are closed tonight, sir.'

Aidan grunted and set off. If anyone was going to touch that creamy throat it would be him and it wouldn't be with his damned mouth.

Cara dodged Martin Ellery's wandering hands yet again and sighed. She'd believed him when he'd said he wanted to see the spectacular view from the highly exclusive, but private, Chatsfield bar—the High Stakes—but even she wasn't usually so gullible. Tonight the bar was closed as all eyes were supposed to be on the casino tables. The quietness of the dark-shadowed open-air bar was somehow more deafening than inside the casino.

Earlier she had felt sorry for Ellery when he'd told her how his first wife had lost their baby in a late miscarriage and how that girl would now be about Cara's age. She wasn't sure of the truth of his story anymore, but it didn't matter because it was clear that all those light touches to her arm and the back of her hand had not had a fatherly intention behind them at all. Somehow, if she hadn't been so worried about Aidan Kelly, she might have picked that up earlier and not found herself alone with him as she was now.

The volcano at the Mirage erupted behind her to the muted oohs and ahhs of the tourists far below, and Cara thought she might erupt, too, if this night didn't end soon.

'I hope you like the view and will come back another time to enjoy the bar when it is open,' she demurred politely, straightening away from the edge of the balcony. 'But now I really have to return to my duties.'

Before the fake smile on her lips had dimmed Ellery grabbed her forearm. 'You know I didn't come out here to look at the view, Cara.' He stepped closer to her and somehow seemed bigger than before. 'Come to my room later on. I know you want to.'

He knew she wanted to?

Cara hoped her disgusted outrage wasn't blaringly obvious as she stared in stupefied silence at him. He might still be considered an attractive man to some women but what on earth had she done to give him the impression that he was attractive to her and, more importantly, how was she going to extricate herself from this situation without upsetting him so much he caused a scene that would get back to Christos?

Feeling as if her mind was a filing cabinet she was riffling through for just the right way to put him off she nearly jumped out of her skin when she felt his fleshy fingers dig into her hipbones, his body trapping hers against the cold metal railing.

'Mr Ellery!' She put her hands up between them. 'I'm seeing someone.'

His eyes narrowed but he didn't move back. 'Who?'

Who? Who? God, did the man not know how to say die?

She glanced desperately towards the main casino doors, hoping like hell someone would come through them and rescue her when he cursed violently, the glow of the fake volcano's erupting flames throwing horrible reddish streaks across his overly tanned features.

'Don't tell me it's Kelly.'

It took Cara a moment to realise he wasn't referring to another woman but *Aidan Kelly*. She paused, her mind spinning. It was clear by the men's interaction—or lack of—at the table that they didn't like each other. At times she'd been sure she'd noticed flashes of almost fear cross Martin Ellery's face when Aidan had won another round. Would it hurt to let him think that she was secretly dating Aidan Kelly? It might mean that he left her alone for the rest of the night. 'A lady never tells,' she murmured, knowing that he would take that as confirmation of his assumption.

'Kelly's a woman hater. Mark my words. He'll break your tender heart, darlin', and bury it along with every other woman's in Australia.'

Considering she had no intention of giving Aidan Kelly the time of day after this horrible evening was over she wasn't at all concerned about her heart—tender or otherwise.

Unbidden, a picture of Aidan Kelly's handsome face came into her mind. When she'd first locked eyes with him at the airport she'd felt as if her heart had stopped beating. As if the ground had moved beneath her feet. Which of course it had because her shoe had been broken, but to her tragically romantic way of thinking he had looked like Prince Charming himself.

He wasn't. She'd known that as soon as he'd growled at her, but it hadn't stopped her from wanting to go out with him. To do more than that, she reluctantly admitted. She had looked at him with the same stars in her eyes that the stewardess had but he had only thought the worst of her and had ignored her ever since. Well, not exactly ignored her. She'd caught him watching her from time to time during the game and it had made her immediately aware of her body in a way that was uncomfortably hot.

And speaking of uncomfortable it was time to stop Martin Ellery's fingers from digging into her waist as if he had a right to have them there. Pressing down on his arms she forced her lips into a smile. 'Look, Mr Ellery—'

'Hope I'm not interrupting anything.'

At the sound of Aidan Kelly's lazy drawl, Martin Ellery released her and shoved her to the side. Cara sighed with relief.

'Well, look who's come to call,' Ellery sneered. 'Lover boy himself.'

Cara made a small strangled noise in the back of her throat she hoped neither man heard. The last thing she needed was for Aidan Kelly to find out what she had let Martin Ellery believe.

And what was it about this man that brought out the worst in her? Or was there a blue moon tonight? Was she going to turn into a pumpkin at midnight?

'You're the one with the moves, old man.'

Cara shivered. The cooler winds brought on by the earlier monsoon had nothing on Aidan Kelly.

'What do you want, Kelly?' Ellery demanded.

'Fresh air,' Aidan said, casually strolling closer. 'Seems I might be in the wrong place.'

'That's because the bar's closed,' the older man sneered.

'Doesn't look that way to me.'

Ellery's eyes narrowed. 'I have to say it was a surprise to see you here tonight.'

Aidan propped himself against the polished balustrading, his lazy gaze taking in the sparkling spectacle of the Strip below. 'Was it?'

The air fairly vibrated with tension but Aidan Kelly, Cara noted, was better at hiding it than his opponent.

Ellery widened his stance. 'You've bitten off more than you can chew taking me on, son.'

With just the barest turn of his head, Aidan's eyes had the arrogant Martin Ellery pinned to the spot like a wrestler on a gym mat. 'Don't ever call me "son" again,' he warned quietly.

'Oh, stop with the intimidation tactics,' Ellery blustered. 'Better men than you have tried to best me before and they've all failed.'

Aidan smiled, more a baring of his teeth. 'I think you're

being a bit paranoid, old man. I came here to play poker. Like you.'

Ellery scoffed. 'Well, enjoy your winning streak. It won't last.'

'They never do,' Aidan drawled as if he felt sorry for the fact.

Cara swallowed. He was a formidable adversary and instinctively she knew that to go up against him would be dangerous. Not that she was intending to if she could avoid it. She hated conflict, much preferring to pull a pillow over her head and hide than have an out-and-out stoush with someone.

Cowardly of her, perhaps, but between the desire to find out how his beautiful mouth would feel on hers and the urge to run for her life, Cara would choose the latter any time. Because, she suspected, if she ever did kiss Aidan Kelly, she'd come out of the experience changed for ever.

Oh, but now that her mind had wandered down that particular track it was hard to pull it back. She wondered what he would do if she asked him to just stand still while she kissed him and then forget it had ever happened.

And where exactly did you leave your brain tonight, you idiot girl? she berated herself. *Because it's certainly not inside your sorry head.*

As if reading her thoughts, Aidan cut his gaze to hers and then let it drop to her lips. They tingled and she felt the strongest urge to part them.

Suddenly she felt very much like the meat in an overcooked sandwich as she stood between the two men.

'Maybe it would be best if we all returned indoors,' she said, knowing it was her job to dispel the sudden hostility that emanated between them.

Unfortunately neither one of them paid her any attention.

'You're out of your depth, boy. Just like your father.'

Cara felt the bite in the air and sucked in a quick breath. She had no idea what the trouble was between the two men but Martin Ellery had just raised the bar if the sudden tension in the man behind her was anything to go by.

Slowly turning around Cara half expected Aidan to have a knife at the ready but instead he smiled benignly at the man who had clearly tried to insult him. Watching him she wondered if she'd imagined the tension she had, moments ago, felt pulsing out of him. Perhaps it had just been her own.

'Gentlemen—'

'You want to be careful, Kelly.' Ellery surprised her by putting his hand back on her waist. 'You might lose more than you bargained for.'

Oh, no. Cara stiffened in mortification at the thought of what Ellery was about to reveal.

'Stop worrying so much, Martin,' Aidan said amiably. 'You're starting to sound paranoid.'

Ellery's hand shook slightly before it tightened on her and Cara did a quick sidestep. If they wanted to butt heads with each other, they didn't need her around to watch.

Before she could make her escape, though, Ellery blocked her way. 'See you at the table, Kelly.'

'I look forward to it,' Aidan drawled.

Ellery glared at him on his way past and completely ignored Cara, leaving her standing on the balcony in a pool of coloured lights with a man who threw off enough testosterone to power the Strip for a year at least.

'So, that was interesting?' she murmured in an attempt to fill the awkward silence.

'Only if you like dirty old men.'

Okay...

'I don't know what the problem is between you, but…

maybe you should go easy on Mr Ellery,' Cara felt compelled to say softly. 'I think he's really scared of you.'

Aidan Kelly didn't move a muscle. 'He should be.'

And so should I, she thought a little desperately.

'*Do* you like dirty old men, Miss Chatsfield?' he asked mockingly.

Try as she might Cara couldn't stop her eyes from taking him in. With his sleeves rolled to his elbows and his formidable shoulders he was possibly the most virile man she had ever seen outside of an action movie. 'Well, that depends on your definition of old.' She smiled to try and lighten the atmosphere. 'But as a general rule I would say not.'

'Then stay away from Ellery. He's poison.'

She paused. The late-night breeze teased the hair at her temples and in the distance the rattle of New York–New York's roller-coaster and requisite screams from the passengers could be heard. She felt flushed even though the night was still cool and her hands had definitely turned clammy.

'Thanks for the warning,' she said as brightly as she could. 'Now, if you'll excuse me I'd better get back.'

Except for some reason she didn't move.

'What did Ellery want?' Aidan asked suddenly.

Cara shook her head. 'Nothing.'

'Nothing?' His blue eyes penetrated deep inside her. 'Are you with him?'

'Am I...' Cara felt her brows draw together. 'As in, am I *seeing* him?'

He waited and she knew that was exactly what he meant. 'No.'

'Do you want to?'

'Absolutely not!' Just the thought of it made her feel ill. The intense man in front of her shifted his weight and seemed to tower over her even though he hadn't really moved. 'Then you shouldn't smile at him as you have been all night.'

Cara frowned. 'I've been doing my job.'

'You've been giving him come-on signals with that smile of yours that promises unparalleled pleasure.'

Cara was shocked by his words. If asked, she would have said her smile had no effect on him whatsoever. But now, with his thick lashes shielding his thoughts from her, she felt an unexpected jolt of sexual awareness deep in her body.

She couldn't stop her eyes from falling to his enticing mouth, the strong column of his neck. It was impossible not to imagine how his mouth would feel pressed against hers because she'd been doing it all night. She imagined he would taste heavenly. Like his scent.

He stepped closer to her, and without meaning to, Cara backed against the wall.

This man didn't have to smile to promise a night of unparalleled pleasure, she thought, he just had to look at a woman. His confidence and subtle air of power were all the aphrodisiac she would need to have her silently beg for him to take her in his arms, to lower his head and kiss her. To have her feel a yearning ache deep in her pelvis she'd never experienced before.

'My smile doesn't—' She stopped when she realised that his eyes were fixed on her mouth. They lingered there before rising to hers, heat radiating from their glittering depths.

'Yeah, it does,' he said gruffly. 'And it might get you what you want with a poor, unsuspecting chauffeur, but a man like Ellery will take it as a green light whether you want him to or not.'

All Cara heard in that statement was the word *chauf-*

feur. 'You know,' she whispered, completely mortified, 'don't you?'

Aidan stepped into her personal space and she had to tilt her head back to look up at him. 'What I know is that you've been driving me crazy all night. Tell me, Miss Chatsfield.' His voice had grown rough and Cara's eyes collided with his. 'Do you deliver on that sex-kitten reputation of yours or are you an absolute let-down when the glamour is stripped away?'

Jolted once again, but this time by the harsh note that had entered his tone, Cara thought that her father would say the latter. Definitely the latter.

Before she could think about how to respond he had stepped closer still. Close enough that she could feel his heat, see the faint trace of stubble forming on his strong jaw. The air grew thick as he studied her, hot prickles of awareness chasing themselves over her cheekbones and down to her lips as if his intense gaze was an actual caress. The inside of her mouth felt like it had never had any moisture in it, and she couldn't move.

His head lowered and every cell in her body sharpened to a single point as she waited for his kiss. Waited for his mouth to touch hers. It was the worst feeling in the world and also the best—that heightened anticipation, that feeling of being poised on the edge of a roller-coaster. You know your stomach is going to flip and you might even feel sick but the thrill of it would be worth it. Worth—

His mouth touched hers. A whisper of contact. Fleeting. Gentle.

For a second they both stared at each other, wide-eyed, their lips barely an inch apart, their warm breaths mingling, and then he moved, wrapping one hand around her waist and anchoring the other in her hair, his mouth slanting over hers with hungry skill.

Cara felt dizzy as the ground beneath her feet tilted and she had to close her eyes and grab on to him for support. Before she knew it his tongue licked along her closed lips and she didn't even think of holding back as she opened to him.

He made a rough sound against her mouth that sent tingles down her spine, and gathered her closer, pressing her breasts into his torso, moulding her lower body to his. He was aroused—and huge—and Cara let out a low moan as his mouth took everything she had to offer.

His lips were warm and firm and then his tongue was in her mouth and—oh, God—sensations zigzagged through her, causing heat to pool at her core. With a small sound she kissed him back and twined her tongue with his, her fingers squeezing his wide shoulders and curving around his neck and into his thick hair. In that moment she could have been anywhere—Paris, Rome…Mars—and she wouldn't have been aware of anything but his kiss.

Unfortunately a loud bang somewhere below startled them both and before she could blink she was free, her breaths coming in short, sharp pants. She pressed her hand to her chest, not unlike the stewardess earlier, and stared at him completely dumbstruck.

His eyes bored into hers, his breathing just as uneven as her own. She stared at the buttons on his shirt, his impressive chest that moved up and down like bellows as he attempted to contain his breathing.

'Meet me later. After the game.'

It wasn't a request, but a command. Rough. Forceful. Exciting beyond measure.

Cara couldn't look away from the burning hunger in his gaze, her blood as thick as treacle as it flowed through her veins. All she wanted to do was lean into him, assuage the hollow ache deep in her body. She'd never had such a visceral reaction to a man before and her mind recoiled from it as much as it craved it.

Her lips buzzed and even though her mind kept telling her that it was wrong, that she should show caution, that she would only get hurt, she took a deep breath and said the only thing that she could.

'Yes.'

CHAPTER FOUR

HAD HE REALLY asked Cara Chatsfield to meet him after the game?

Aidan couldn't quite believe it. But there was no doubt that the blood still hummed through his veins and once again he had to force his mind away from that kiss and back to the whole purpose of his being here.

Kissing her had been a spur-of-the-moment thing and he just didn't do those. Everything in his life was planned out to the nth degree. His housekeeper often teased him about it, but secretly he knew she loved how orderly his life ran. 'Like clockwork,' she'd chortled more than once.

Yes, like clockwork. Just the way he liked it. He liked knowing that there were no nasty surprises around the corner. Nothing that would throw him off track. And why was he thinking about such things right now? Now when he needed his mind razor sharp and focused.

And okay, he found Cara Chatsfield attractive, but so what? He'd found women attractive before and never been controlled by his libido like that. So she smelled pretty and she had a small brown mole beside her right ear. Really what she was was a piece of fluff.

And no matter how beautiful the package he wasn't a man who would ever be interested in someone who was fundamentally untrustworthy. Even short term.

Cara Chatsfield was too young, too wilful and most likely too shallow. What was annoying to him—no, what was appalling—was that given all that he knew of her reputation he also knew that he would still meet up with her later on. Still take her to his bed. For some reason she… *Fascinated* was the wrong word, but he couldn't think of what the right one was to describe how he felt about her.

Basically, he couldn't take his eyes off her. Like now. She was talking to one of the bartenders across the room. Annoyingly she had barely come close to the main table since their run-in out on the balcony. And what a thing to call it. He could have laughed. He'd followed her out, come over all superior about Ellery and ended up pressing her into the wall and losing his head. *Nearly* losing his head, he amended.

He recalled the way Ellery had been holding her when he'd stepped through the terrace doors. Cara's brief look of relief. She'd said they weren't lovers and that she wasn't interested in Ellery but why hadn't she slapped the other man's face? And why even think about that? Her response was her own business, not his. The fact was, he wasn't her keeper and she and Ellery weren't lovers. He didn't need to know anything else about her to enjoy the promise of those feminine curves. And nor did he want to. Pleasure was all this was about.

Abject pleasure.

And maybe he'd organise a late supper for them both back in his room, have a drink together and then…then they'd have sex. It would be great if that kiss was any indication and then…then he'd wake up tomorrow, fly to the conference his company had organised in Fiji and that would be the end of the delectable Miss Chatsfield.

The back of his neck ached and he heard it crick as he eased his shoulders. The barman she was talking to was

about her age. They'd probably watched the same kids'
programs.

Kids' programs?

Hell of a way to win a poker game, Kelly, he admon-
ished himself. *Real sharp.*

His eyes cut across the table to Ellery, who was straightening one of the few remaining towers of chips he had left.
This was why Aidan was here. This man. Or more spe-
cifically, to ruin this man, and if that somehow brought
a sour taste to his mouth, then…who cared? He'd made a
promise to his dying father that he would destroy Ellery,
and Aidan always kept a promise. The fact that his father
hadn't *requested* the promise just showed Aidan how dam-
aged he had been by Ellery's deceit because, really, his father should have gone after the man himself for what he'd
done to him. Instead he'd bailed out on life.

Hell.

Aidan swiped a hand through his short hair as a line
of sweat trickled down the back of his neck. A woman's
laughter drifted across the room. The sound husky, sexy.
Cara. He made a fist with the hand that had held the nape
of her neck, his body recalling how silky smooth her skin
had been, how the sinuous length of her had fit so damned
perfectly against him. How the taste of her had been so
damned fine.

'Mr Kelly?' The croupier recalled his attention back to
the cards. 'The bet is now with you.'

Ruthlessly reinstating his ironclad powers of concentra-
tion Aidan breathed deeply and tuned Cara Chatsfield and
everyone else out. He had a good hand. A winning hand.
And unless he was mistaken about Ellery's tell, he didn't.

With only the Korean furniture magnate, who had already bowed out of this round, left at the table after five
hours of play, Aidan decided it was time to go in for the

kill. Especially since he could feel his lack of sleep creeping up on him. Better to preserve what energy he had left for more pleasurable pursuits than this one.

'I'm all-in.' He shoved his pile of chips into the centre of the table amidst gasps from the small crowd that had gathered around.

Martin Ellery looked back at him through eyes gone a little wild. A pretty normal reaction when earlier he'd stupidly used his company as collateral to buy extra chips and he had little left to show for it.

The man was staring down the barrel of absolute ruin and Aidan was holding the gun. And he couldn't have felt better.

Finally, after years of watching his father fade away before his eyes, Aidan was going to enjoy watching this bastard squirm.

Ellery's upper lip twitched almost imperceptibly but Aidan didn't know if that was because he was scared or angry. Cara's soft words about going easy on Ellery came back to him and he ruthlessly shut her voice out. She had nothing to do with this. Nothing.

Minutes ticked by as Ellery contemplated his move and the small, fascinated crowd pressed closer.

'Come on, Ellery,' Aidan snapped. 'Call or fold.'

Ellery stared down his nose at Aidan and pushed the rest of his chips forward. 'I'll raise you.'

Aidan snorted. He gave the man's meagre chips a cursory glance. 'You'll need more than that to stay in the game, old man.'

'You're a bastard, Kelly.'

'Actually, I had a father.' Aidan's tone hardened until it could have decimated granite. His heart shrouded in ice. 'Now, correct me if I'm wrong.' He frowned as if confused. 'But you've already staked your business, the family cattle station and the company jet. So what else have you got up your worthless sleeve, old man, that you could possibly raise me with?'

Someone gasped but Aidan didn't care. His attention firmly focused on the wounded animal in front of him.

Ellery swallowed, the full import of Aidan's intentions registering on his pale Botox-heavy features and Aidan felt victory course through his veins like a caffeine rush. This was what he had waited so long to achieve. Martin Ellery on the ropes. A smirk crossed Aidan's face as the moment of truth neared, his gaze lazy and predatory as he watched the older man. 'Come on, Ellery,' he drawled. 'What else you got?'

Ellery's gaze briefly shifted to the bar and his face took on a smugness his situation didn't warrant. 'I got something, Kelly. Something I know you want.' His gaze cut to Cara Chatsfield, who was now looking across at them, her lower lip caught between two straight white teeth. 'I've got *her*.'

Aidan felt his brow furrow. 'What are you talking about?'

'A night with Cara Chatsfield. That's what I'll raise you with.'

Aidan's first thought was that a night would be nowhere near enough with Cara Chatsfield.

His second wasn't so pleasant.

Ominously the events of the evening crystallised in his mind like ducks lined up at a shooting range. The Chatsfield socialite running into him at the airport, his hijacked limousine, her request for him to go easy on Ellery. That kiss. Had it been to distract him?

Another glance towards the bar revealed that she was still looking his way. Her eyes wide, and from where he sat it looked like her breathing had suddenly grown shallow as if in anticipation of later on. Give the girl an award, he thought acidly, she certainly knew her game.

Aidan's gut knotted and the word *fool* ricocheted inside his head. Yes, he'd bet that kiss had been nothing more than an attempt to throw him off his game, and it very nearly had.

Anger surged through him. Anger that he'd almost been played.

'Meet me later. After the game,' he'd said like some eager beau.

'Yes,' she'd breathed as if she couldn't wait.

What a joke. And, unfortunately now that he had worked out exactly what was going on, the joke was on them, not him.

Aidan forced his features to remain impassive but inside fury had strung his muscles tight. Why hadn't he considered all this before?

Because he hadn't been able to shift his mind from sex every time he looked at her, that was why.

Well, she'd certainly put paid to that. He wouldn't touch her now in a New York minute.

Cocking his eyebrow as if in weary amusement he forced an easy laugh. 'Really?' he drawled, focusing entirely on Ellery. 'You're going to have to do better than that.' He had Ellery's head on the chopping block; there was no way he would concede to him now. 'You can't meet my bet with a woman.'

'The rules of the house say that you have to accept any wager I propose, boy,' Ellery said with cocky self-assurance.

'Any wager that's reasonable. Yours is ludicrous. Now find something else.' Aidan's tone hardened with every word. 'Or fold and pray you have a friend whose couch you can sleep on tonight.' He'd waited a long time to strip this man of everything he owned and nothing but his absolute—and very public—humiliation would suffice to make Aidan feel that his father had finally been avenged for the wrongs perpetrated by his once-good friend.

A piece of weighty jewellery clunked as a woman raised her arm, the sound elevated by the anticipatory stillness in the room.

The old man fidgeted, sweat beading his brow. The background noise from the bar filtered into Aidan's consciousness. 'You're done for, Ellery,' he said softly. 'Admit it.' The moment of victory was so close he could taste it. So why did he feel so tense? Shouldn't this moment of triumph relieve him of this unbearable burden? Make him feel light? Make him feel *happy*?

Cara Chatsfield mistakenly chose that moment to step slowly onto the dais, her lovely face a mask of innocent concern. Did she know her lover had just wagered her? Was this something else they'd concocted together outside on the balcony?

Then it struck him. It hadn't been relief he'd seen on her face when he'd approached her and Ellery before; it had been fear. Fear that they'd nearly been caught out.

Logic told him it wasn't possible. That it was all too elaborate. But logic wasn't ruling him right now. Instinct was and his instincts told him something was amiss. That something had been amiss from the moment she had stumbled into him hours earlier.

'On second thoughts,' he found himself saying, 'I'll take your bet.'

Then he'd take her. So fast and so hard she'd rue the day she'd ever tried to cross him.

Cara knew something wasn't right as soon as she approached the table.

She hadn't been near it since she'd returned from outside, Aidan Kelly's kiss on the terrace crowding her mind.

At the time she'd been too mesmerised to pull away. His heat, the sheer maleness of his lean, muscular body so close to hers, the intense way his gaze seemed to eat her up. She'd been so enthralled she hadn't even tried to ward him off as she would have done any other man she barely knew.

Instead she remembered moaning and then she'd felt the hard thrust of his arousal against her belly. She'd felt dizzy, excited. The danger signals and the loud beating of her heart had drowned out everything other than him. Including common sense!

But could she really meet up with him later on? Could she really go through with it? Have sex with a stranger? A stranger whose car she had 'borrowed'...

Or maybe this was fate.

Because how else to explain how right it had felt to be held close in his arms. How else to explain the open hunger she had seen in his face that must have surely been reflected in her own?

So why wouldn't he look at her now?

Icy fingertips stepped slowly down her spine. Something was wrong, something was very wrong.

She'd sensed it from across the room, in the stillness in the air. It was what had drawn her back to the table. Now she wished she'd run in the other direction.

She noted Martin Ellery's pallor and Aidan Kelly's warriorlike expression. Despite the fact that he was slouched back in his chair he looked like a weary despot with a thousand men to back him up.

The woman beside her let out a shaky breath and threw Cara a sympathetic look.

Unsure, Cara smiled at her. 'What's going on?' she murmured. 'What are they betting on?'

The woman raised both eyebrows and let out a shaky laugh. 'You.'

'Me?' Cara could barely get the word out and her eyes flew to Aidan's. His expression was thunderous, accusatory—as if this was her fault!

'Are you serious?' she whispered to the woman.

'Oh, yes. The older man suggested it.'

Ellery?

Cara swallowed, a sick feeling balled in the pit of her stomach. 'And…and the other one agreed?'

'Just then.'

Oh, God. Why? Why would Aidan agree? And what on earth was going on in Martin Ellery's head for him to suggest such an inconceivable notion? What could she say to get out of it? As if in a warning an image of her father shaking his head with resigned disappointment came into her mind. If she caused a scene now he'd think she had done it deliberately. He might even think it was her idea! Her way of having fun…

Unsure of how to extricate herself from what felt like a very volatile situation, she didn't say anything.

Which seemed to give Martin Ellery a victorious cue to crow, 'She'll do it!'

All eyes turned back to her expectantly. Cara froze. What could she say? And surely he was only talking about dinner. Like when she'd allowed herself to be part of a charity auction to raise money for the homeless. That had cheapened her enough in her father's eyes. Tonight, though, Cara felt that she was damned if she did and damned if she didn't.

'Well…if you're talking about my company for—'

'Done.' Martin Ellery thumped the table in an aggressive show of machismo. 'Show your hand, Kelly.'

Aidan Kelly's low growl as he sent his cards spinning across the table sent a shiver of alarm down her spine.

He wouldn't look at her and Cara's mouth went bone

dry. He looked so hard the hairs on the nape of her neck stood on end. This was not the man who had kissed her senseless outside before, the man who had gazed at her as if she were the only woman in the world for him.

She wondered what she would do if he won. Then a worse thought hit. She wondered what she would do if Martin Ellery won.

Oh, God.

'Mr Kelly has a straight flush,' the croupier announced in his perfectly modulated tones. 'Mr Ellery, your cards please.'

Cara saw Ellery blanch and he almost seemed dazed as the croupier retrieved his cards and sorted them.

She felt a buzzing in her ears as she waited. She could feel people's curious eyes on her and she knew a dull flush had heated her cheeks.

When the croupier sorted Ellery's cards into the line-up a groan went through the swelling crowd and Cara tried to make sense of them. Four queens... Did that mean Ellery had won or lost?

'Mr Ellery has four of a kind.' The croupier paused and Cara half expected to hear a drum roll. 'Mr Kelly wins.'

Mr Kelly wins?

It took a moment for his words to sink in and when they did Cara's head came up and her eyes locked with the man she had only hours before agreed to meet up with for a late-night assignation. His face was hard, the angles seeming to sharpen as he stared at her with retribution burning in the hot depths of his blue gaze.

His expression confused her.

He looked at her as if he knew she was a world-class stuff-up. A fraud. A person who, once you scratched the shiny surface, had no worthy place in the world.

'Tell me, Miss Chatsfield. Do you deliver on that sex-

kitten reputation of yours or are you an absolute let-down when the glamour is stripped away?'

Aidan stood up straight and tall, lording it over those around him. His eyes narrowed and he swept the table with a contemptuous glance. 'You can have your precious company, Ellery, and your contaminated money. I don't want any of it.'

Ellery stared at Aidan like a broken man who still stood facing the hangman's noose. 'You're letting me keep... *everything.*'

Aidan's lip curled. 'Almost.' His eyes cut to hers and Cara felt pinned by his glacier-blue gaze. 'Everything except her.'

CHAPTER FIVE

AIDAN WAS FURIOUS. Bitterness rolling through him like a steam train. And not only bitterness, but a deep uncertainty he didn't want to acknowledge. Why had he just thrown everything back at Ellery? Why had he just walked away without exacting his revenge?

He didn't know, but he did know that he was shaken by the whole experience. Shaken by the woman at his side. Shaken by her kiss, her innocent expression, her lies.

And now she really would pay. Oh, not with her body. He no longer wanted that. No, he'd teach her a different lesson for taking him on.

She stumbled as they crossed the Mahogany Room in full view of the spellbound crowd and he tightened his grip on her elbow.

'Smile, my lovely,' he whispered down at her. 'Everyone will think you're not looking forward to the night ahead.'

'Mr Kelly—'

He stopped and curled his mouth into a grim smile. 'I think we've gone way past the *Mr Kelly* stage, don't you? In fact, I'm wondering if we shouldn't give everyone a peek at your performance out on the balcony. From what I saw on that music clip you're quite the exhibitionist.'

'No, I—'

Aidan yanked her towards him and her small, icy hands splayed over his chest.

'Then keep moving,' he growled low enough that only she could hear him. 'Or I'll forget all about being civilised and lift your skirt and take you up against the nearest wall.'

She turned white and he told himself he didn't care. That she didn't deserve his gentleness or his consideration. He reminded himself that she had agreed to put herself up as a lure and unfortunately for her she had caught the wrong fish.

Without another word he pulled her into the lift and swiped his key card over the console to take them to the presidential suite.

Ignoring the way her fingers twisted together he pulled her into his room and kicked the door closed behind them.

'Mr Kelly, please—'

'It's Aidan, doll face, and if you're really lucky, then, yes, I will please you.'

She hovered in the middle of the silk-carpeted room. 'If you would just let me spea—'

'I don't want you to speak,' he snarled. 'I want you to strip. And do it slowly.' He smiled. 'I want to enjoy every minute.' He relaxed back on the king-size sofa and stretched his hands along the backrest and watched her. 'Leave the stockings and heels on.'

She looked unsteady on her feet. 'You can't be serious.'

'Oh, I am. I've thought of you bent over my dining room table in those heels and nothing else all night and I can't wait for the real thing.'

The silence that followed his deliberately crude statement was loaded and he waited to see what she would do. Waited to see just how far she had agreed to go.

* * *

How had she ever agreed to meet this cold-eyed stranger for sex? Cara thought numbly, the hot, savagely pleasurable kiss on the balcony like a distant memory.

Dry-mouthed she stared at him, her mind blanking out as she tried to calm her beating heart long enough to think. He couldn't mean it, he just couldn't, and yet…she couldn't see an ounce of mercy on his hard face.

She didn't know how to placate him and she shook her head. 'I can't,' she said, swallowing around the croak in her throat.

'You need a drink first?' His eyebrows rose with mocking sincerity. 'I confess I didn't think it would be necessary considering you knew the score.'

'Look, we didn't work anything out downstairs,' Cara began. 'I didn't actually agree to…sex.'

'You allowed yourself to be bet on in a poker game. Did you think it was just for dinner? Some polite conversation?' His voice turned hard. 'Maybe you thought we could sit around discussing the latest movie showing in the cinemas?'

'I can see you're angry, but—'

'Oh, I'm not angry. I'm excited. Not every day a man wins a woman in a poker game.'

'That wasn't real.'

It had been the wrong thing to say; she saw that immediately and took a shaky step backwards as he leaned forward, his elbows balanced on his wide-spaced knees.

'Lady, I had a lot riding on that bet. I had Martin Ellery in the palm of my hand.' He slapped the back of one hand into the palm of the other. *'The palm of my hand,'* he roared. 'He was broken. And once again you're there interfering. Making it possible for him to win. If he had, if he had won…'

For a brief moment the air became charged with something other than menace. Cara's gaze stayed pinned on Aidan's. *Was it...pain?*

She should have been scared and she was, but she also understood that whatever was going on between them it had more to do with the man he had left beaten and broken downstairs. 'Why are you so upset with Mr Ellery?' she asked softly. 'What did he do to you?'

'As if you don't know?'

Cara shook her head. 'I don't.'

He rose slowly from the sofa and came towards her. 'You're good. I'll give you that. I believed everything you said out there on that balcony.'

Cara backed up nervously. 'I didn't lie.'

He kept on coming as if she hadn't spoken. 'I believed you hadn't encouraged Ellery. I believed he was in the wrong. But the car. The balcony scene. The bet...' He gave a harsh bark of laughter. 'I tell you, you really had me going for a while.'

'You knew about the car.' Cara stopped moving and cringed. 'Oh, God. I knew you knew.'

'But you weren't going to tell me, were you? You weren't going to apologise for stealing it.'

'I didn't steal it,' she spluttered. 'I borrowed it.'

He leaned against the edge of the table in front of her and crossed his arms, a bemused expression on his face. 'Borrowed it?'

Cara wasn't fooled by the supposedly relaxed stance; he looked like he'd be on her in a second if she said one wrong word. Her pulse was racing and she took a deep, calming breath. 'What I did was wrong and I fully admit that. At the time it was raining and I knew I'd never make it to the hotel on time and...I'm really sorry. I would never normally do anything like that but I was tired and stressed and…' She groped for more words as his expression grew bored. 'I was—'

'Selfish?' He cut through her stammering apology. 'Wilful? How about spoilt?'

'Angry with you, if you must know,' she snapped.

'Ah, now the truth comes out.'

Cara took a deep breath. Really, there was no good fighting with this man; she'd seen how that had gone down for Martin Ellery.

'Mr Kelly—'

'Come on, baby, surely you can call me by my first name. Especially after the way you gazed at me outside before.'

'I didn't gaze at you,' she denied.

He sneered. 'You not only gazed at me but you parted those sweet lips for my kiss.'

'I didn't… I didn't want you to—'

He pushed away from the table and slowly stalked towards her. 'You wanted me to. You wanted me to kiss you and a whole lot more. And you will again.' He stepped closer and Cara collapsed back onto the sofa chair she had unwittingly backed into. 'You'll give me everything you would have given your lover and more.'

Her lower lip trembled as it had a tendency to do when she was truly upset and she set her teeth into it. Hard. 'He's not my…my lover.'

He leaned forward and caged her into the chair with his hands on either armrest. 'You play a good game, doll face. I think Ellery should have sat you at the table tonight. He might have fared better. But the jig is up so stop lying to me.'

Cara felt the press of the cushioned seat against her back. 'I'm not lying to you. I don't know what you're talking about. I told you outside I wasn't seeing him.'

'I love the wide, innocent eyes,' he said conversation-
ally, his gaze raking her face insolently. 'They're a nice
touch.' She saw him glance at the hands she was wring-
ing in her lap and she stilled them. 'They're a nice touch,
too.' His eyes drifted down her legs and then slowly back
up. Shockingly his gaze warmed her and she felt the air
between them become charged with something other than
anger.

'Look, I made a couple of mistakes today,' she said
appealingly. 'I should never have gone to L.A. I see that
now. Even though it was to thank my agent. Probably I
was thinking that things seemed to be going too well for
me. That something had to happen. And so I created it. I
mean, something always goes wrong. Of course, I didn't
know that the flights would be delayed but—'

'What the hell are you talking about?'

'Me.' Cara felt the last of her control unravel as a tear
slipped over the edge of her eyelashes. 'I'm a disaster.'
One tear followed the next and she buried her face in her
hands. 'Bad things just ha-ha-happen to me and—I know,
I know—it's my f-fault. I…'

Aidan watched appalled as the beautiful girl on the sofa
dissolved into tears before his eyes.

He tried to make sense of what she had just said but
he couldn't. But it did give him pause. All that blubber-
ing about not going to L.A. and things going wrong and
being late… He was starting to think that maybe he'd been
wrong. That maybe she'd been as much a victim of Ellery's machinations tonight as his family had been fourteen years ago.

Was it possible?

Hell.

Aidan watched the tears slip down her face and her

attempts to control them and the hard wall that had surrounded his heart since she had been offered up as a stake started to crumble.

He hadn't meant to make her cry. If he was honest, he'd expected her to offer herself to him. He'd expected her to start stripping. Then, when she was halfway through, he'd been going to shake his head, look at her with the disgust she deserved and throw her out.

And yes, he'd meant to scare her, as well. Just a little so she'd think twice about doing something so foolish again. Think twice before putting herself in such a vulnerable situation.

'Well, mission accomplished, boy.'

Martin Ellery's voice filled his head and he made a low growl. He was not like that man and he never would be.

He saw Cara jump and he automatically reached for her. She flinched as he gripped her shoulders and tried to pull away but Aidan eased her up. Then he did something he hadn't even realised he'd intended and sat down and pulled her into his lap.

'Shh, Cara. It's okay. You don't have to be scared.' He stroked his hand over her back. 'I'm not going to hurt you. Just relax.'

Gradually he felt the stiffness ease out of her and as her sobs subsided she curled more tightly in his arms.

Then she eased back and looked at him.

'You're right,' she said, sniffing and swiping at her eyes.

Aidan reached for the box of tissues on the low table beside them. He held one to her nose. 'Blow.' She took it and tried to tend to the damage on her face. Her eyes already slightly red and puffy. Clearly the woman was not a good crier. And why did that thought make her even more appealing?

'I'm not sure I want to hear what I'm right about,' he said gruffly.

'I—I did gaze at you outside. I did want to—want to kiss you.'

Oh, hell. Did she have to go and remind him of that while she was so warm and pliant in his arms? While her bottom was nestled so sweetly against his groin?

Arousal followed swiftly on the heels of that awareness and she must have felt his body harden because she went still. Then those green doe eyes dropped to his mouth.

Aidan swore silently and tried to still the blood pounding through his veins.

He had not brought her up here for sex. He hadn't… 'Cara, you're…you're…' Now *he* was going to start stuttering.

'I'm…I'm what?'

Oh, to hell with it, he thought. To hell with the whole damned night. He wanted her. Why keep denying it? Especially when she looked at him as she did now. As if she wanted him, too… His hand came up to cradle her head and his mouth lowered to hers at the same time. Longing and a desperate urgency rushed through him as his lips met hers and his hand tightened in her silky hair. The driving need to take her shocked him with its urgency and it took every ounce of willpower he had to keep from forcing his way into her mouth to take the sweetness he'd tasted earlier.

Somehow he waited. Nibbling and sipping at her lips until he felt them soften. Until he felt them give beneath his own and then he couldn't wait any longer. 'Open your mouth, Cara,' he urged. 'Let me in.' She made a small whimper as she obeyed and Aidan felt like he was experiencing his first ever kiss as he slipped his tongue into her warm, wet mouth.

He groaned and banded his free hand around her waist, pulling her torso flush against his own. She tasted of coffee and dark chocolate and sweetly of herself. Her hands found his shoulders and she clung to him, her body arching into his in a way that was sheer bliss.

The need to touch more of her raced through his blood and he bent her back over his arm and cupped a firm breast in his hand. She moaned his name, her hands clutching his shoulders, her body arching into his as he kissed and licked his way down her smooth neck.

She writhed in his arms and gripped his head as his mouth moved lower. He slid his other hand down over her shoulder and dragged the top of her dress with it.

She was wearing a lacy peach-coloured bra and the tips of her breasts were already distended and tight with anticipation. Cupping them both he plumped them up and dragged his thumbs across both nipples. She gasped and then cried out when he replaced his thumbs with his mouth, greedily lathing first one tip and then the other through the soft lace until she was frantic and twisting in his arms.

The taste of her blew his mind and he completely lost his head as he shifted her bra aside and sucked one stiff peak deep into his mouth, working her aroused flesh with his teeth and his tongue. She pushed hard against him and he guided her up on his lap until she was nearly straddling him.

Just when he was about to shove her fitted skirt to her waist so he could place her legs either side of his thighs, Ellery's voice sounded inside his head again. *'Way to go, boy. You got further than I did.'*

Aidan briefly closed his eyes and pushed his head back against the sofa. Cara's body followed and he placed his hands at her waist to hold her back.

'Stop.' He shook his head to try and clear it. 'Cara, stop.'

'What?' She gazed at him, her lips bruised and swollen, her eyes unfocused.

Aidan swore and lifted her off him as he pushed to his feet. He left her perched on the edge of the sofa and stalked towards the wet bar.

A crystal decanter sat on a silver tray with six matching tumblers—he didn't care if it was full of motor oil. He needed something to dull his senses and bring his mind back online so he yanked the lid off and poured a healthy measure.

'Aidan?'

Now she said his name.

He lifted the glass and tipped the contents down his throat. He waited two seconds for the burn to hit his gut and then he poured another.

Shifting his gaze to the oval mirror behind the bar he saw that she had risen to her feet, the top of her dress thankfully pulled back into place. Her face and upper chest were flushed with desire and her short hair was mussed from where he'd thrust his fingers through it.

Damn, she looked beautiful.

She pressed her swollen lips together tentatively and something like guilt twisted inside him. He hadn't meant for things to go that far. Well, he had, he conceded; he'd meant for them to go much further. Before the bet.

Ellery's ugly mug jumped into his mind and his gut churned with the need to forget every single thing about this night.

'You need to go.'

He hadn't turned to face her and her cheeks flamed with embarrassment. He watched her eyes climb up his back and her lower lip started to tremble when she saw that he was watching her.

'But I thought…'

Aidan slammed the crystal tumbler down onto the wooden bar, cutting off whatever it was she had thought. He was hanging on to control by a thread and he wanted her gone.

'Doll face, I don't really know what you thought but you need to grow a brain. You do not hijack people's cars because you're in a hurry, you do not let yourself be bet on in a game of high-stakes poker and you do not come to strange men's rooms and... Do not start crying,' he bellowed as a fresh spill of tears trekked down her face.

Bloody hell, but those tears tore something up inside of him.

Without thinking he started towards her only to have her throw her hands up in front of herself. She looked touchingly vulnerable with her feet apart and a fierce expression on her face, her slender frame trembling as if she really did have a chance of stopping him. She wouldn't, of course. She wouldn't have a hope in hell of stopping him from doing whatever he wanted to do if he had a mind to.

'Don't come any closer.'

'I don't intend to,' he said softly. 'The door is behind you. I suggest you use it.'

'With pleasure.'

The silence in the room after the dull thud of his door closing was loud and oppressive.

Aidan moved to the plate-glass windows and stared outside.

The Strip beckoned like a shiny toy hiding a tarnished interior. Flashes of red, green, blue and gold. Flashes of pink. All of it designed to lead a man to his downfall.

If he let it.

CHAPTER SIX

Cara hated early mornings as a general rule and she particularly hated them after only two hours' sleep, most of which had been spent crying.

Crying because she felt sorry for herself.

And she still didn't know how one of the worst nights of her life could also have some of the best moments in it. Or how a man who so clearly hated her could have made her feel so…so…aroused.

So desired.

So *wanted*.

It was a true testament to her desperate state of mind that she could even think that Aidan Kelly had wanted her with any of the urgency that she had felt for him.

It was the way he had held her when she'd burst into tears that had lowered her defences towards him. His gentleness coming so quickly on the back of such coldness. It had made her let her guard down. It was exactly what she'd wanted her father to do on the rare occasions that she had seen him while she was growing up. A nugget of affection to help her through the lonely times.

She closed her eyes and groaned softly as the memory of Aidan Kelly's hands and mouth on her body rushed through her. She'd never been kissed like that before. As if the man she was with couldn't get enough of her. And, even more surprising, she'd never felt like that when a man had kissed her before. As if she was no longer in control of her own body. Her own mind.

The whole night had been like that noisy roller-coaster two doors down. The thrill followed by the spill.

His kiss had been unforgettable and yet she wondered if he truly believed that she wasn't Martin Ellery's mistress. It seemed important that he did, though she couldn't think why. She would never see him again, after all.

Oh, she felt awful. Embarrassed by her physical reaction to him. Mortified by his total rejection of her. The way he had just been able to push her aside and stroll to the bar as if nothing had happened. The way his cold eyes had met hers in the mirror. God, he hadn't even bothered to turn around to talk to her face-to-face.

Remembering that she had switched her phone off when she'd collapsed into bed a short time ago she switched it on. Nine messages pinged into her inbox. She counted three from Christos, another three from Cilla, one from her friend Lucy and two from her agent.

A horrible premonition made her skin suddenly feel damp and she clicked to open the first one from Christos with mounting unease.

From: Christos.Giatrakos@TheChatsfield.com
To: Cara.Chatsfield@TheChatsfield.com
Subject: URGENT!

Call me.

Well, that told her absolutely nothing. She clicked on the next.

From: Christos.Giatrakos@TheChatsfield.com
To: Cara.Chatsfield@TheChatsfield.com
Subject: URGENT!

Immediately.

A man of few words.
Then she flipped to a text from her sister.

Hope UR ok after last night. Call me. Xx

Cara suspected she wasn't referring to Aidan Kelly's kisses, which was just as well, because she might never be okay after those again.

Worried that the cryptic messages were alluding to the poker game, Cara clicked onto her internet connection and searched for her own name.

What she saw made her want to bury her head in the pillow and never come up for air.

Cara Chatsfield Game for Anything.

Cara Chatsfield Caught in a Three-way.

A three-way!

Chatsfield Wild Child Staked by Aidan Kelly.

Oh, great.
Cara was about to throw her phone on the bed when her agent's name flashed up on the screen.

She didn't answer it. She knew she'd be upset with her. Ever since she'd been in that rock video a year ago Harriet had warned her she had to clean up her act or she'd never be offered a decent job again. But she'd also taken her on after she'd sacked her previous agent and told Cara that she believed in her and that she'd work damned hard to turn her career around. Cara knew that Harriet had put her own professional reputation on the line for her, and now this.

She clicked on the message and it felt like a cement brick had landed in her stomach when she read it.

From: Harriet.Harland@TheHarlandAgency.com
To: Cara.Chatsfield@TheChatsfield.com
Subject: What the hell???

Demarche furious. Just pulled your contract.

This is bad.

Call me. Hx

For a moment Cara's mind went completely blank.

She tossed her phone on the bed as if it had just bitten her. She felt numb. Winning Demarche had been a huge coup and now it was gone. And she'd really wanted it. Initially she had fallen into modelling because of her face and her name. It had been fun having all those people fuss over her, telling her she was beautiful. Telling her that she was fantastic, *daaarling*. It had been so different from growing up between a remote manor house and a boarding school full of girls who would just as quickly cut you off at the knees as draw you into their fold.

What she had come to appreciate was the craft of modelling. Of learning how to show the clothes she was wearing in the best light. Fashion had become a sort of passion and she loved having a hand in what she was wearing.

Demarche had offered something more, though. They

had been offering her a role as not only their house model, but as a spokeswoman for the company. A representative of their brand. They had been offering her credibility and the opportunity to be part of something bigger than herself. A place to belong.

Now they were offering her nothing and it was all her own fault.

Feeling the threat of tears again, Cara determinedly dashed them away.

This was not the time to crumple. This was the time to pull herself together and…do what?

Run home with her tail between her legs?

Run home to her flat and her friends who would jump up and down in outrage for her right before they passed her a margarita. And she didn't even like margaritas!

But she didn't want to talk about last night. Certainly not to her friends because they wouldn't understand.

Lucilla might, but she knew Cilla had her own problems to deal with right now. As did her brothers, and she didn't want to hear Antonio tell her again that she needed to take responsibility for her actions. She *knew* she did.

And no doubt the press would camp outside her doorstep again 24/7 and hound her mercilessly. It was what they did best in the UK. So far the paps in the US didn't seem so bad.

No. Going home to England humiliated and fired wasn't an option.

Nor was staying here.

She officially hated Vegas now.

Pulling herself out of bed she headed for a steaming shower and wondered what Aidan Kelly thought of all the publicity surrounding last night. Of the photo she had seen of him dragging her out of the Mahogany Room. Damn mobile phone technology anyway.

No doubt he'd hate it. No doubt he'd already be making a statement to distance himself from her as quickly as possible. It's what her father usually did.

Wanting to burst into tears again she bit into her quivering lip and wished she'd emptied the minibar of champagne when she'd returned to her room last night instead of chocolate. That way maybe she wouldn't remember everything so clearly. That way maybe she might still be asleep.

Maybe she could hide out in some hippy artist colony in New Mexico and learn how to make Aztec jewellery, one of her recent passions.

Only the papers would no doubt publish that she had been in rehab. And why did she care so much? Well, for one, because she was tired of people suggesting that she coasted through life because of her name. Tired of being labelled the bad girl of the family. Somehow the bad-boy reputations of her twin brothers—Orsino and Lucca—were revered. Hers was issued as a subtle put-down and last night Aidan Kelly had made her feel cheap.

She wasn't. She'd had two lovers in her life—though no one would believe that.

It wasn't fair.

Nothing was fair.

Cilla would tell her to stop being 'so sensitive' but Cara couldn't help it. She didn't know any other way to be.

Feeling trapped and maudlin, she decided to go to the airport and look at the destination board and pick the place farthest away from anywhere else.

As far as plans went it wasn't much of one and…who was she kidding? She hated being alone and she knew that if she was she'd relive every moment of last night over and over until the only place she'd be fit for was an asylum.

Quickly texting Harriet she asked her agent if she could crash on her couch for a couple of days. It was the safest place she knew at this point in time even if she would have to explain everything and probably grovel. Harriet responded with an immediate yes, but somehow Cara didn't feel any sense of relief.

She's going to be so disappointed in me.

Trying not to picture her agent's face when she arrived, and wondering which parts of last night she would share with Harriet, she stuffed clothes into her suitcases, wishing she'd packed a little lighter for once. The one thing she could never tell Harriet about was how Aidan Kelly had kissed her and touched her last night. Or how much she still craved the touch of a man who didn't even like her. There was pathetic and then there was *pathetic*.

And as much as her father might think that she was worthless, she knew deep down in her heart that she wasn't. That she just felt a little…lost sometimes. As if she didn't belong anywhere.

Not wanting to dwell any more on negative thoughts Cara pulled on loose linen pants and a singlet top. Her Jackie O sunglasses would hide the fact that her eyes looked ravaged from lack of sleep and too much crying and a baseball cap would help cover most of her hair to stop anyone from recognising her.

Then she closed her suitcases and dialled down to reception.

If she hadn't been so sleep deprived and preoccupied with her problems she might have been more prepared for the wall of paparazzi that surged towards her as soon as she stepped outside of the hotel.

But she wasn't prepared at all and before she had time to blink she found herself backed up against the glass wall and her cap and sunglasses knocked to the ground. Quickly bending to retrieve them she shielded her eyes from the prying lenses of the cameras.

Wedging her glasses back into place she stood up and tried not to appear as if she was cowering. But she was and the barrage of reporters had her perfectly trapped as they pitched questions excitedly at her head.

As a general rule Aidan was an early riser. It was a habit he'd established the day he'd taken over his father's business.

He usually started the day with a session in his gym, or a run around the Sydney Botanical Gardens near his home. Then he'd return, have a shot of espresso his housekeeper would have prepared and take his chauffeur-driven car to work.

In the old days, in the beginning, he'd have driven himself to work. His first car had been a late-model powder blue sedan—as ugly as they came and he'd hated it. He used to dream about the day it would be turned into a Ferrari. Fire-engine red. Why go for the discreet black or sunflower-yellow. At the time he'd wanted bright *and* bold. Out there.

Somehow he'd never gotten around to buying that Ferrari. Why own a car you didn't have time to drive?

He frowned. The Merc made more sense. He could make phone calls in it, work on his computer, or take a meeting if he was in a rush. Hell, he'd even had sex in his limousine one night when he'd been pushed for time and his lover had begged.

He remembered now that he hadn't enjoyed the experience that much. Not like last night.

And what the hell was Cara Chatsfield doing in his head again?

His frown turned into a scowl. She was like a sore that wouldn't heal. A painful one. He never should have touched her. How many times had he told himself that already? How many times had he told himself that one taste of her honeyed charms had been more than enough?

Last night he'd been so tied up in his need for revenge that he'd become almost paranoid. He hadn't been able to see what was real and he still wasn't sure he knew. All last night had revealed was that the issues of his past hadn't felt lifted when he'd beaten Ellery and he'd taken that out on Cara.

Did he owe her an apology? Probably. Would he see her again to give her one? Probably not.

And what was she doing back in his head again? Because Aidan knew better than anyone what happened when you took your eye off the ball.

Yeah, you do stupid things like let Ellery off the hook.... Sighing heavily he thought that maybe he should go for a swim in the hotel pool before he left. He glanced at the bedside clock. 7:00 a.m. Hell, he didn't think he could drag himself out of bed if the hotel was on fire. So far he had seen every hour and half-hour since he'd dropped into bed two hours ago.

Frustrated with himself he swung his legs out of bed just as his mobile phone rang. It was the senior editor of his biggest newspaper. Since she rarely had cause to contact him he picked up.

'Dana, what's up?'

'Well, good morning to you, too, chief. You sound like you've had a hard night. Not that I'm surprised.'

A sense of foreboding slid down Aidan's spine. 'What are you talking about?'

'Your big night with Britain's wild child. Everyone here is truly peeved that you let the competition get the exclusive. They are blowing us out of the water already.'

'I didn't have a big night with anyone,' he lied.

Dana reeled off some of the morning headlines and

Aidan felt completely stupid for not anticipating that this would happen. The room had been half filled with patrons at the time of the bet. It was a pretty good indication of how unlike himself he was right now.

Hell.

He wondered how Cara was faring this morning and then once again reminded himself that she wasn't his problem. And no doubt she was lapping up the attention. It was what women of her ilk got out of bed for. Attention and notoriety.

Which suited him just fine because they were the two things he liked the least. He knew the celebrity-hungry press wouldn't bother him with any questions because they likely knew he'd get them sacked.

'Do you want me to make a statement?' Dana asked.

As much as he hated the thought of the publicity he'd garnered from last night he knew the best course of action was to say nothing. 'Just ignore it.'

It was, after all, what he himself had decided to do about the whole thing.

CHAPTER SEVEN

Having organised his car to pick him up at the rear security exit of the hotel Aidan stepped into the lift and turned his back on a young couple kissing passionately in the corner. Fools, he thought, and absently noted that the colour of the flowers the girl clutched were a deep pink. Almost the same colour as Cara Chatsfield's hair.

When he realised where his mind had led him he couldn't believe he was *still* thinking about her. It was out of control. It had to be the guilt over reducing her to tears the night before because it couldn't be anything else.

Unlike Casanova beside him, he didn't have a romantic bone in his body. He stood still as the youth whispered, 'I love you', over and over into the giggling girl's ear. Ah, young love. Thank God he'd had his eyes opened before he made a fool of himself like that poor schmuck.

The lift doors opened and he couldn't get out of there fast enough. His account would already have been settled so the only thing to do was to walk out. Walk out and forget last night had ever happened.

And he would have done exactly that if he hadn't been confronted with the vision of the woman he was trying really hard not to ever think about bailed up against the external glass wall of the hotel.

She had one hand on her face and the other out in front

of her as she tried to force her way through the pack of baying paparazzi with minimal success.

Aidan swore violently, his strides eating up the space between them in a matter of seconds.

Shoving his way through the pack just as a security backup team arrived to control the situation, Aidan pulled Cara into his arms.

With her hands over her glasses she didn't know it was him and she resisted, trying to twist out of his grasp.

Or perhaps she resisted all the harder because she did know it was him, he thought ruefully. After the way things had ended between them last night he wouldn't have been surprised.

'Sweetheart, it's me,' he crooned loudly enough for the closer reporters to hear. 'Sorry I kept you waiting. If I'd known you were going to be attacked like this I would never have let you come down alone.'

She stilled and lifted her face to his, her lips pressed together in a quivering line.

Knowing he couldn't cope if she burst into tears again he did the only thing he could think of. He ducked his head and put his mouth against hers. It was the briefest of touches, meant to reassure her that he was on her side and nothing more. He hoped she read it that way because his body wanted to take the kiss deeper and keep on going.

Feeling her body sag he bent to her ear. 'Put your arms around my neck.'

She did, clinging to him for support, and then she was in his arms and he was carrying her back inside, her head tucked firmly under his chin.

Aidan threw the remaining paps a fulminating glare as he walked past and he didn't stop until he was back in his room and had quickly deposited Cara on the deep-seated sofa.

She sniffed and gazed back at him with angry tears streaming down her face.

'Here.' He handed her a tissue and repeated his command of the night before. 'This is becoming a habit. Blow.'

She sniffed again and took it, swiping at her eyes beneath her sunglasses before doing as he'd instructed.

'Are you okay?' he asked briskly.

'No...not really.'

Aidan paced away from her. 'What the hell happened down there? I thought you'd be used to handling those types of situations.'

She sat up straighter and folded her long legs underneath her. 'I mistakenly thought the US press were nicer than the UK ones and I...I wasn't thinking very clearly when I left my room.'

He shook his head. 'No paparazzi are nice.'

'You must think I'm pathetic,' she murmured.

He scowled but didn't answer her. She looked like a scared kitten that had just been plucked from its mother to be sent home with a new owner.

'This is awful,' she murmured. 'I take it you know what the papers printed about last night.'

'My senior editor rang this morning with the wonderful news. She wanted to know why I'd let the other papers have the exclusive.'

Cara gave a watery smile. 'What did you say?'

'Nothing. I don't play into trashy gossip.'

'Lucky for you because I hate to think about what they're going to print after the way you just swooped in and rescued me. They're going to say we're a couple. Why did you do it, by the way?'

Good question, he thought. And one he didn't have a readily acceptable answer for. And worse still, he hadn't thought about how his actions would be perceived. He hadn't thought about anything other than getting her out of harm's way.

'You were in trouble and no one else was helping. I would have done the same for anyone.' Which was possibly true. 'And why do you care so much about what the press think?'

She swiped at her face with the damp tissue. 'I don't.'

'Then why are you crying?'

'I'm not.'

'You are,' he said patiently. 'And you clearly care.'

'Well, so would you if you'd just hit rock bottom.'

Thinking that she was probably exaggerating he crossed his arms and tried not to look exasperated. 'Why have you hit rock bottom?'

She frowned. 'I was supposed to be on my best behaviour last night and this morning I sent a text telling Christos that I would stay out of sight until this whole thing blew over and he's going to be so mad at me now because there will be even more pictures of me and—'

'Take a breath, Cara. And who the hell's Christos? A lover?'

'No.' Her eyes briefly dropped to his mouth and then just as quickly found the carpet between them. 'Christos Giatrakos. He works for my father. He's my boss. Sort of.'

'Your boss?'

She let out a worried sigh. 'He sent me to hostess the high-rollers room last night so that I could contribute to the family business with the specific instructions to not cause a scandal.' She gave a little hiccup and told him the rest, including losing her lucrative deal with Demarche, the French cosmetic giant. 'This might be one of my worst scandals to date. Put up as a stake between two men. God...' She dropped her face in her hands. 'I'll never work again.'

'You won't if you keep crying,' he growled, absently

wondering what it was about this woman's tears that moved him when usually a woman crying left him feeling like they were trying to emotionally manipulate him. An impossible task since he didn't do emotions.

Somehow, though, he knew Cara Chatsfield's tears were genuine and he felt sorry for her.

'I can't help the way I feel,' she blurted out. 'And I don't understand why you're not furious.'

'Stories like this are a dime a dozen.'

'Maybe. But you're not the one they're implying is a cheap tramp. The guy's reputation never suffers in this situation. In fact, you just come out looking more virile and attractive. But me…' She swiped at her eyes hidden by truly ugly sunglasses and her lips quivered as she fought back more tears.

And *still* he found her somehow alluring.

'Have you eaten?' he asked abruptly.

She glanced up at him. 'What has that got to do with anything?'

Not bothering to answer he stalked across the room and picked up the hotel phone. 'Coffee, some pastries, bacon, eggs, toast and whatever headache tablets you have in this country.'

'Why did you order all that?'

'It's harder to cry on a full stomach.'

'Is it?'

Aidan ran a hand through his hair. 'I don't know, but it will help your headache.'

She looked startled. 'How did you know I have a headache?'

One corner of his mouth kicked upwards. 'The tablets were for me.'

'Oh.'

His smile grew at her contrite expression and he realised

that ordinarily he'd be pissed at having his well-ordered life disrupted like this but for some reason he wasn't.

'But you keep rubbing the back of your neck.' And it was truly distracting him. 'You just need to relax. This will all blow over before you know it.'

Her mouth twisted as if she didn't believe him. 'For you, maybe. For me…last night is just one more notch on my bad-girl belt. And I have no idea what to tell Christos now. He's already left a couple of filthy messages on my phone this morning and that was before this latest disaster.'

Aidan rubbed the back of his own neck then. He'd meant to help her before, not make it worse for her, and he felt another twinge of guilt about last night. He knew he could have rejected Ellery's suggestion of putting her up as a stake but he hadn't. For the first time in his life he'd ignored logic and felt a primal rage that he had been made a fool of. Something that turned out not to have been true.

But if he was honest, that hadn't been the only thing driving him last night. Once his mind had locked on to her and Ellery as a real couple he'd wanted to rip her away from him. He'd wanted to rip her away and lock her in a room and ask her how she could have been so stupid.

But perhaps she wasn't the stupid one in this scenario. Perhaps he was.

Aidan wrenched at the collar on his shirt, unused to feeling like he wasn't in control of a situation.

'If you think about this logically,' he began, deciding it was time he did that very thing. 'What happened downstairs actually plays to your advantage.'

She sniffed. 'I don't see how.'

'That's because you're being emotional. Think about it. I know of Christos Giatrakos. If he thinks that we're actually involved he'll be more relieved than not. You can tell him this whole thing was misinterpreted, we're a couple and no harm done.'

She chewed on the inside of her lip and Aidan forced his eyes to meet hers. Only, she had on those damned plastic sunglasses.

'Take them off.'

She paused and her throat bobbed as she swallowed. 'Take what off?'

Your clothes. Take off your clothes so I can see you again. Touch you. So that I can lay you out flat and taste every inch of you.

Aidan stilled as images of Cara in his arms downloaded inside his head like an X-rated movie. Man, but he had to get out more.

'Your glasses.' His voice sounded like it had rolled across sandpaper. 'I can't talk to you with those damned glasses on.'

Cara felt her body shudder at the rough timbre of his voice and she wondered if he hadn't read her mind. If he hadn't known that all she could think about with him pacing in front of her was how lethally attractive he was. Tall, masculine and so powerfully self-assured. He had swept her up in his arms before like a white knight and her girlhood fantasies about being saved like some princess in a fairytale had been reborn.

Stupid, worthless fairytales. They had clearly been written by people with wild imaginations and no life to speak of. A bit like herself right now…

'I need them on.'

Aidan stopped in front of her. 'Why?'

'My eyes are sore.'

Before she could stop him he had reached forward and slid them off her face. Cara quickly ducked her head but he

gripped her chin. She shivered and closed her red eyes, trying to push his arm away. It was like trying to bend steel.

He swore and released her.

'This has really upset you.'

He thought she'd been crying so desperately over the
publicity, she realised, something that was infinitely more
preferable to what had really made her so upset last night:
his rejection and how much of a failure she felt.

'Yes.'

'Hold on.' He gripped her chin again and brought her
eyes back to his. 'Your eyes are blue today, not green.'

'Violet actually, though you probably can't tell because
they're bloodshot. I'm wearing coloured contact lenses and
channelling Elizabeth Taylor to cheer myself up.'

Aidan hesitated as he took her in. 'Do you actually need
contact lenses?'

'No. I just like them.'

'What colour are your eyes naturally?'

'A boring colour.'

Before he could respond and tell her that he doubted that
there could be anything boring about her at all there was
a discreet knock at the door. Aidan dropped her glasses
into her lap.

While he moved to answer the door Cara jumped off
the sofa and raced for the nearest room.

His bedroom. It still smelled faintly of his spicy scent
and she told herself to ignore it. To ignore every sexy
thing about him.

She glanced in the mirror to find that her eyes were
slightly less puffy than before but that she had been right:
they were still a little bloodshot. Combined with the flush
on her cheeks she looked a real treat.

'Cara. Where are you?'

'In here.' She reappeared in the doorway and tried to

seem more together than when she'd first arrived. Aidan stood beside a linen-covered trolley laden with food and her stomach growled. 'I didn't want the room service person to see me.'

He gave her a sardonic smile. 'I think it's a bit late for that, don't you?'

He held out a cup of coffee. 'How do you have it?'

'With arsenic.'

His smile broadened and her hand shook as she took the cup from him and added milk and sugar. Did the man have to look so together in his suit and pressed shirt? He made her feel like a wilted flower by comparison.

'Surely it's not that bad,' he said.

'For you,' she reminded him glumly. 'I still have to work out what to tell Christos.'

'Don't tell him anything.'

'Easy for you to say.'

'Then tell him we're a couple and last night was some sort of wild sex game.'

'Unfortunately he would believe the latter of that bizarre statement but not the former.'

'Why not?'

'You need to ask? The respectable Aidan Kelly and the Chatsfield disaster, a couple? I don't think so. No.' She shook her head automatically as he handed her headache tablets. 'I'm a health nut. I prefer to heal naturally.'

'Very admirable. Now take them.'

She rolled her eyes but did as he bade. 'Are you always this bossy?'

He hesitated briefly and then shrugged. 'Apparently, yes.' Then he handed her a croissant.

'I don't eat anything with butter, either.'

'That's ridiculous. No wonder you cry so much.'

She smiled at that and eyed the pastry. She hadn't had

a buttery croissant in years. Her stomach rose in anticipation and he thrust the plate closer. The yeasty scent went up her nose and she took it rather than argue.

'Listen,' he began. 'I can't help feeling slightly responsible for the bind you're in and I'm serious about you telling Christos that we're a couple.'

'Don't you care about what people will say about you?'

'I can hold my own in the world, Cara.'

His use of her name made swallowing the strip of croissant she'd peeled off difficult and it felt like paper in her dry mouth. She gulped down a coffee chaser and cleared her throat. 'He'll never buy it.' And when Aidan showed up in the papers in a week's time with a beautiful woman on her arm she'd feel even more like a fool. 'So thanks, but I'm good.'

'Good?' He looked dubious. 'What's your alternative?'

'I was thinking of spinning a globe, closing my eyes and pointing and then just disappearing for a while.'

'On your own?'

She shuddered. 'You're right, bad idea. I'll hide out at my agent's house in LA instead.' Not that she really wanted to because Harriet would want to plan her next move and as far as Cara was concerned her next move was to make like an ostrich.

'That's it.' He gulped down the espresso he had poured himself and set the cup down on the table. 'You're coming with me.'

Cara stared at his frowning face. 'Where?'

'I have a conference for the next two days in Fiji. You can come, sit on the beach, go to the spa. Give yourself a couple of days to come up with a better plan than globe spinning.'

She gave a faint smile. 'What will that solve? You hate me.'

'I don't hate you.' He paced across the windows and

stared outside. 'And it will make our relationship look real enough for Christos to cut you some slack.'

Great, he felt sorry for her…but Cara had to admit that the thought of laying low on a tropical island held a wealth of appeal.

'Will there be any paparazzi there?'

'It's an exclusive resort that values the privacy of its guests. And I'm not taking no for an answer.'

Cara looked at the man opposite her. He was throwing her a lifeline and she knew she should feel better about it than she did. Could she spend the next two days in the company of a man who attracted her more than any man ever had before?

'Do you ever?' she asked.

'No.' He smiled and her stomach somersaulted.

Which was when she knew that if he ever did decide that he wanted her she would be in massive trouble.

CHAPTER EIGHT

LANDING IN FIJI, Cara was immediately struck by how different it was to Las Vegas.

Where Vegas had been full of flashy lights surrounded by empty desert, Fiji was understated but completely lush. There was no other word to describe the deep green of the tropical foliage, the spicy-sweet humid air and the deep blue waters of the South Pacific.

They arrived in late evening and by the time they had reached the speedboat that would take them to their island destination the hot ball of the sun had dropped below the horizon. Darkness followed quickly behind and by the time they were seated on the white leather bench seats and their bags stowed the stars were already twinkling in a black velvet sky, so close it was as if Cara could reach up and touch them.

She felt the wind whip through her hair and the spray of water on her face as the speedboat roared across the warm ocean and skirted small, darkened islands, some lit from within by tiny dots of yellow lights while others lay eerily pitch-black. All were ringed with pale white sand and edged with gently swaying palm trees that seemed to stand as silent centurions shielding a tropical interior.

Not for the first time Cara wondered if she'd made the right decision coming with Aidan. Although the opportunity to hide out from her problems had been initially appealing Cara couldn't shake the uneasy feeling that she should have just returned to LA or London and the fold of her friends. At least with them she would have been too busy to get caught up in thinking about what a disaster zone she was.

Looking around her now she was uncomfortably aware that she was going to have to spend vast amounts of time alone or with a man who had kissed her breathless and already found her wanting.

The speedboat slowed as they neared an island that looked like it had come straight out of *Robinson Crusoe*. A line of waist-high torches lined the sandy shore and disappeared into tropical undergrowth and small boats were pulled up onto the sand. The only sounds Cara could discern were the putting sounds of their engine and the swish of the water as it rolled onto the shore.

Suddenly she had a horrible vision of being stuck on an island all by herself with no one to talk to and just the memories of how much she had mucked up last night to keep her company.

A large native man on the beach raised his hand and yelled a greeting as he waded into the water and grabbed the prow of their boat.

'Is it always this quiet?' Cara murmured as Aidan came up beside her.

'At this time of the night, yes. You better take off your shoes and roll your pants. We have to wade in.'

'Oh, right.' She peered over the side at the swirling water. 'They don't have biting fish in Fiji, do they?'

'Only piranhas, but they sleep at night.'

Cara glanced up in time to see a quick grin fade from his lips. 'Very funny.'

She handed over her handbag and sandals to the waiting boatman and slipped into the warm, shallow water.

Aidan rolled up his pants and leaped with easy grace into the shallows, as well, and Cara mused that there was no way the man could spend every day sitting in an office chair and running a multi-billion-dollar business.

'Are you sure the conference is here?' she asked.

'What's wrong?'

'I can't hear anything except the trees moving and the water breaking on the beach. And it's so dark. Sort of eerie.'

'Don't tell me you're afraid of the dark?'

Feeling completely exposed by his flippant tone Cara turned her head away and concentrated on not stepping in any unseen holes in the sandy shallows. She nearly jumped out of her skin when she felt Aidan's hand on her elbow. The chemistry she'd been trying to ignore flaring hotly to life inside of her.

'You *are* afraid of the dark.'

'Not the dark per se...' She swallowed. 'I have a phobia about being alone.'

His brows rose up his forehead. 'A phobia?'

'Well, it sometimes feels like a phobia. I just like having people around. When I was little I used to climb into my sister's bed most nights to sleep.'

'Not your parents'?'

'No. They weren't really around much.'

He looked at her curiously and Cara turned away. She never spoke about her parents—or lack of them.

'*Bula.* Welcome to the Coconut Beach Front Resort.'

'Thank you.' Cara turned to smile at another Fijian man who greeted them. This one was the size of a sumo wrestler but his open smile was instantly engaging.

'Dinesh!' Aidan greeted him like an old friend, giving the man one of those high manly handshakes she had seen her brothers do together when they hadn't seen one another for a while.

'Good to see you again, boss. It's been too long.'

Boss? Was that some sort of friendly island greeting, or was Aidan literally the man's boss?

'Dinesh, this is Cara Chatsfield. She is my guest while we're here.'

'A pleasure to meet you, Ms Chatsfield. I hope you enjoy your stay.' He turned to point a little way up the beach. 'If you would please come this way I'll drive you to your bungalow.'

He led them to a small buggy and within minutes they had pulled up outside a quaint wooden beach hut with a thatched roof. Cara was completely charmed as she made her way up the couple of steps to a wide veranda.

Another native Fijian, a woman dressed in traditional island sarong-style skirt and white blouse, handed them a tall glass of fruit juice and Cara sighed blissfully at the flavour, feeling a renewed sense of energy as the sugar hit her system.

Inside, quaintness gave way to decadent luxury with whitewashed walls, deep-seated sofas and dark wooden floors covered in traditional hemp rugs. Exotic flowers had been placed around the large living area and Cara stepped into the small tub of fresh water to rinse the clinging sand from her feet before venturing inside.

'Oh, this is really lovely.'

She turned and then stepped back to let Dinesh pass with their luggage.

Unexpectedly large hands spanned her waist and she let out a nervous sound as she realised she'd stepped straight back into Aidan. For a heartbeat her bottom nestled against his hard thighs and Cara forgot to breathe as heat rushed through her body.

She took a quick step forward and his hands dropped to his sides. 'I'm sorry,' she said, her voice slightly hoarse.

'My fault,' he intoned, not looking at her as he moved farther into the room. It seemed to Cara that the previous night hung between them as if no time had passed at all and she didn't know whether to move forward or backwards. Both physically and metaphorically, she thought without real amusement.

Deciding to explore while Aidan spoke with Dinesh, Cara discovered an ornate gold-and-marble bathroom straight out of a Turkish bathhouse, two single bedrooms and a larger bedroom with a huge four-poster bed fit for a queen.

A low hum of pleasure lingered on her lips and, grinning widely, she made an elaborate circle with her arms when she heard Dinesh behind her with the bags.

'Dinesh, this is—'

Cara's eyes widened and she dropped her arms awkwardly to her sides. Instead of Dinesh it was Aidan and he was scowling at her.

'Your bags.'

'Oh, thanks.' Not wanting him to think that she had automatically expected to take the master bedroom and doing her best not to imagine what it would be like to actually share the room with him, Cara cleared her throat. 'You can have this room. I didn't expect—'

'That's fine.' He cut her off. 'I don't sleep much anyway.'

Needing to get away from the big bed and him, Cara made the mistake of moving at the exact moment he did, but this time rather than just brush against him she found herself momentarily plastered up against the front of him.

'Oh, I'm so sorry.'

Heat didn't just simmer this time, it shot through her, and the breath that hitched in her lungs sounded like a gunshot in the quiet room. Aidan's blue gaze burned into hers and Cara felt her pulse leap as she held her breath in anticipation of his devastating kiss.

Only instead of kissing her, Aidan pressed his lips together in a grim line and clamped his hands on her shoulders to push her back.

'Get some sleep.'

He strode out before she could make another objection and, feeling totally despondent at yet another rejection, she made her way to the bathroom. She gazed longingly at the sunken bathtub but opted instead for a quick, refreshing shower before climbing into bed.

An hour later, as exhausted as she was, it seemed her body was confused by yet another sudden change in the time zone and she was unable to sleep. Unable to stop thinking about how many people she had inadvertently let down last night.

Rolling onto her back she stared at the pale curtains tied back at each post and listened to the unfamiliar island sounds outside her windows. She wondered if Aidan was asleep and then made a face in the darkness.

Well, of course he was. He'd had as little sleep as she had and would no doubt be as efficient in sleep as he seemed to be in everything else. She almost suspected he could command himself to sleep and he would obey. There were not many men who had that kind of powerful aura, not even her father.

She thought about how in the early years at school the girls had gossiped behind her back about why her mother had left and who her father's latest lover was. At the time Cara had mistakenly believed that she was in competition with those women for her father's affections but in the end she had learned the truth. There hadn't been any competition at all because she hadn't stood a chance.

Hating that those thoughts kept creeping into her head all of a sudden when she usually had no trouble keeping them at bay, she pushed the bedcovers back and stood up. The reason she usually had no trouble keeping them at bay was because she was always busy. Busy having a meal with friends, shopping, dancing… Her life was a blur of activity and this silent, remote island was making her feel even more alone.

As was the big empty bed.

Since trying to will herself to sleep wasn't working, Cara decided that a glass of warm milk might help.

Tentatively she opened the bedroom door and as quietly as possible tiptoed down the short hall and into the main room.

She had imagined that Aidan would be fast asleep but he wasn't.

He was up. Slouched on the sofa wearing an old T-shirt and grey sweatpants. His short hair looked like he had run his hands through it one too many times and his computer was open on his lap.

He looked sexy and rumpled and her stomach did a silly little flip just looking at him.

'I'm sorry,' she said on a rush. 'I didn't know you were up.'

Aidan felt his whole body tense as Cara hovered in the doorway. It was difficult to make her out in the low-lit room but unfortunately not so difficult that he couldn't see that she was wearing some sort of pale nightgown with shoestring straps. A pale, *short*, nightgown that, combined with her short, straight hair, reminded him once again of a cute, erotic pixie.

'What do you want?'

He saw the way she recoiled at the harshness of his tone and felt like a jerk. Unfortunately she'd appeared just as he was questioning his reasons for leaving her bedroom earlier without doing anything about the hunger that had surged between them.

Something at the time had held him back, something in her expression that had given him pause, but looking at her sexy body now he couldn't bring to mind exactly what that was.

'I'm sorry, I didn't mean to disturb you.'

'You're not,' he said smoothly, wondering when he'd become such a good liar. 'What's wrong?'

'I couldn't sleep and thought I might fix myself a warm cup of milk. It used to work when I was a child.'

'Fine.'

Still she hovered at the edge of the room. 'Look, I probably don't need it so I'm sorry for—'

'Would you stop saying sorry,' he growled.

'Sorry.'

Realising what she had just said she smiled. 'Oops, so— I mean, not sorry.'

Aidan felt a reluctant grin tug at the corner of his mouth and her smile widened.

'Get your cup of milk.'

'Thanks.'

She moved towards the small open-plan kitchen and he told himself to return to the spreadsheet on his computer screen before he forgot what it was he was working on.

'I didn't really get a chance to thank you for helping me earlier because you were working on the plane but...' She tucked a strand of her hair behind her ear. 'I feel really bad that I've imposed on you.'

'Forget it. I was the one who made the situation worse.'

FREE Merchandise is 'in the Cards' for you!

Dear Reader,

We're giving away FREE MERCHANDISE!

Seriously, we'd like to reward you for reading this novel by giving you **FREE MERCHANDISE** worth over **$20**. And no purchase is necessary!

You see the Jack of Hearts sticker above? Paste that sticker in the box on the Free Merchandise Voucher inside. Return the Voucher promptly...and we'll send you valuable Free Merchandise!

Thanks again for reading one of our novels—and enjoy your Free Merchandise with our compliments!

Pam Powers

Pam Powers

P.S. Look inside to see what Free Merchandise is **"in the cards"** for you!

We'd like to send you two free books like the one you are enjoying now. Your two books have a combined price of over $10, but they are yours to keep absolutely FREE! We'll even send you 2 wonderful surprise gifts. You can't lose!

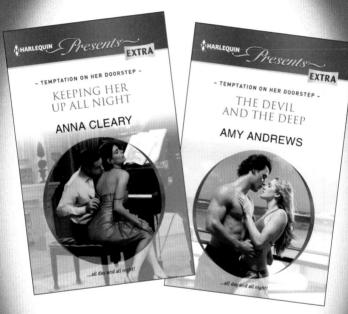

YOUR FREE MERCHANDISE INCLUDES...

2 FREE Books **AND** 2 FREE Mystery Gifts

Detach card and mail today. No stamp needed. ▶

FREE MERCHANDISE VOUCHER

2 FREE
BOOKS
and
2 FREE
GIFTS

Please send my Free Merchandise, consisting of
2 Free Books and **2 Free Mystery Gifts**.
I understand that I am under no obligation to buy
anything, as explained on the back of this card.

❏ I prefer the regular-print edition
106/306 HDL GEHZ

❏ I prefer the larger-print edition
176/376 HDL GEHZ

Please Print

FIRST NAME

LAST NAME

ADDRESS

APT.#   CITY

STATE/PROV.   ZIP/POSTAL CODE

NO PURCHASE NECESSARY!

HP-714-FM13

'You were only trying to help me and I appreciate it.'

'Good. Glad that's straightened out.'

'I just—'

'Has that milk boiled yet?' he asked brusquely.

'Oh.' She whirled around to the stainless-steel stovetop and checked the pot.

Aidan nearly groaned as her short skirt flared around her hips. He wondered what she would do if he walked up behind her and slid his hands around her small waist and pressed up against her. Before he could contemplate if he might actually follow through with that thought she turned and poked a wooden spoon in his direction.

'See, I don't get that.'

'Get what?' he asked warily, hearing the plaintive complaint in her voice.

'One minute you're nice and then the next you're not.'

'It's not you.'

She snorted. 'Now you sound like you're breaking up with me.'

Aidan stretched his legs out in front of him, giving up on the spreadsheet. 'It's-not-you-it's-me type thing?'

'Exactly.' Her smile lit up her face.

'Used that line a lot, have you?'

She grimaced. 'More like that line has been used on me.'

Aidan's eyebrows shot up. 'You're kidding?'

She shook her head. 'Unfortunately not. Lucilla has a theory that I date all the wrong kinds of men because I want them to reinforce my view of the world.'

'Which is?' Aidan's eyes slid over her. He thought about all the reasons he shouldn't go to bed with her and couldn't come up with one. Yes, she was young, undoubtedly frivolous and impulsive, but so what? He didn't want to marry her. He didn't want to marry any woman.

'She thinks that I've been let down by love too many times and now I only choose men who can't commit.'

His eyes met hers. That just about summed him up.

'Interesting,' he murmured, surprised to find that he actually was. 'And what do *you* think?'

She shrugged as if the whole topic meant very little to her. 'I think that if there is a social climber or a social misfit within a ten kilometre radius, then I could find him if I was blindfolded and tied to a post.'

Aidan laughed with genuine amusement. 'I can see why you thought you might damage my reputation. I've never been called a social misfit before.'

Cara giggled. 'Well, obviously fake relationships don't count.'

'Lucky for me.'

'That's what I was thinking. So what about you?'

He looked back at her uneasily. 'What about me?'

'You don't have a girlfriend right now, do you?'

Aidan raised an eyebrow. 'I would hardly have brought you with me if I did. But no, women don't seem to hang around long enough to become girlfriends.'

She tilted her head and her hair caught the light from the nearby lamp, the soft glow casting a strange intimacy over the room that was disconcerting.

'Why not?'

This time he was the one who shrugged as if it didn't matter. Only for him it really didn't. 'They say I work too much.'

'And do you?'

She glanced at his computer in his lap and he laughed. 'Possibly.'

Cara pointed the wooden spoon at him again. 'See, now, I have a theory about that.'

'Another theory?' Wondering why he was still sitting

on the sofa with a hot woman in the kitchen bantering with him Aidan seriously contemplated pushing his computer off his lap and replacing it with her.

'Yes. I have a theory that when you meet the one—you know, that perfect person just for you—then you can't not be with them.'

Aidan fought back a wry smile. 'Drop everything, you mean. No work, no sleep, no food. Just twined in each other's arms for ever and ever.'

'No, of course not. I meant that you love that person so much you can't bear to be away from them.'

'True love,' he mocked.

And there was the reason she was still across the room and not in his lap. The sixth sense that had stopped him from hauling her into his arms in the bedroom doorway and utilising that made-for-sex mouth of hers: she wanted everything he avoided. His worst nightmare of a woman.

She pouted. 'You're making fun of me.'

Surprised to find that he felt a little hollow from the revelation he'd just made about her, he smiled faintly. 'Just a little. But are you seriously telling me that you only date men you think are going to be the one?'

'Well, I don't go out with men I think *aren't* going to be the one.'

And by that token she probably didn't sleep with them either. Had he so completely misjudged her last night? 'How's that milk coming along?' he asked, desperate now to have her return to her room.

'Oh!' She yelped and pulled the pot off the stove. 'I forgot about it. But it's okay.' She looked up at him. 'Do you want one?'

Aidan shook his head, bemused to have even been asked. 'I'm good.'

'It will help you sleep.'

Only a knock to the head would help him sleep after seeing her in that silk nightie.

'So I take it you don't believe in true love and have never been in love,' she said.

He forced his eyes up from her small, high breasts. 'I've dated a lot of women in my life and I can assure you that I've been happy to see every one of them go.'

'Which proves my theory.'

'I don't see how but, pray, enlighten me.'

'You've never been in love and you've always been happy when a relationship has ended. If you'd ever really been in love you wouldn't be so happy right now.'

'You're right,' he said coolly. 'I'd be miserable instead. But I have to ask. Were you in love with that artist you ran off to Ibiza with when you should have been sitting your A-levels?'

He could see the question had shocked her but he needed a reminder of the kind of woman she really was, not the one she was intent on presenting to him.

'I know the papers said I went there *with* the artist, but I didn't. I went there *for* an artist.'

He shook his head as if that distinction was hardly worth noting. 'I hope he was worth it.'

'It wasn't like that,' she said, a dull flush of colour highlighting her magnificent cheekbones. 'I didn't *know* him personally. I went to Ibiza to see his work because he was truly inspirational and he was dying. That exhibition was his last one and at the time I thought it was more important than a maths exam.'

Seriously unsettled by his lack of control over his libido Aidan didn't want to hear her excuses. 'Well, now you know better.'

'Yes. Now I know that no matter what you do in life, if you make a mistake it will hang around like a bad smell and no one will forgive you for it.' She placed her cup carefully on the bench. 'I know you live your life completely mistake free, but the rest of us aren't so lucky. We do things wrong occasionally. But the other thing that I know is that if everyone in the world forgave others for their inadequacies and their mistakes instead of trying to mould them into something they find acceptable, the world would be a happier place. It's people who let pain turn into resentment and anger who do the most damage.'

She looked slightly embarrassed by her outburst and her lower lip quivered and made him feel like a heel. 'Just go to bed, Cara.'

Outrage shone out of her eyes and for a minute he thought she might put him in his place for being such a judgmental fool but she didn't. Instead she bid him a stiff good-night before walking off with her nose in the air.

Aidan released a long breath. It had been a long time since he had sported a boner from just looking at a woman.

And now he realised that as well as trying to stop her tears and help her out earlier in the day by bringing her to Fiji, he'd also had an ulterior motive. He'd brought her here with the possibility of finishing what he had started at the casino the other night.

Her diehard belief in love and happy-ever-afters meant that his conscience was unlikely to let him follow through on that because he had nothing to offer her.

Which left him stuck on an island with a hard-on and a true romantic.

Great.

These next few days were likely to be a lesson in restraint. Something he should excel at.

The only bright spot he could see in having her around was that she took his mind off Martin Ellery. In fact, he hadn't thought about the old man and how he had failed to carry out the revenge he'd harboured for so long since he'd dragged her out of the Mahogany Room and that was the way he wanted to keep it.

CHAPTER NINE

'GREAT KEYNOTE SPEECH,' Ben James, Aidan's second-in-command and long-time friend enthused. 'You were right to bring him in to do it. I had no idea Smithy was so insightful.'

'Glad you enjoyed it.'

Aidan, himself, hadn't heard anything past the opening joke. And now they were walking towards the next session and he had no idea which one it was.

Ordinarily he would sit in on one or two but this morning he couldn't seem to concentrate.

Cara's outburst the night before had both surprised and disturbed him. He'd known immediately that she hadn't been just talking about the social fabric of the world they lived in but something far deeper. It was in the flash of vulnerability when she'd believed he was judging her. He hadn't been. Not initially. He'd been honest when he said that her bad-girl reputation didn't bother him. What did bother him was the stab of jealousy he had felt when he'd imagined her blissfully happy while she was coiled around some dodgy artist on a sun-soaked futon. The image had rocked him and then he'd taken the double hit of being faced with her trembling lower lip. That sure-fire sign that she was hurt twisted his insides into huge knots.

Which was why the less time he spent with her the better because not only was his emotional and physical reaction to her a shocking thing to witness, but her talk about forgiveness had sliced something open inside of him. Like a scythe through the very heart of his memories.

Forgiveness was not a concept he'd spent a great deal of time dwelling on before. His father, now that he thought about it, hadn't been a forgiving man. He'd harboured a justified hatred of Martin Ellery right up until he had died and often bitterly pronounced that he just hadn't seen it coming.

Now, looking back, Aidan wondered if not only had his father not forgiven Ellery, but if he'd never forgiven himself for not noticing what had been happening right under his nose. Had he stopped living, stopped functioning as a man, because of that one simple flaw? And what did it say about Aidan, himself, when he had taken up the mantle of his father's resentment?

And why was he suddenly questioning himself now?

Cara Chatsfield, that's why, he realised darkly. *Talking to her was just as dangerous as looking at her.*

The beat of the sun high in the sky made its presence known as soon as he and Ben exited the main building. The soft sandy path and lazy insects buzzing around the exotic plants making a mockery of their suits and black leather shoes. They should be wearing shorts and flip-flops. Casual wear, like the surfer who just passed them on his way to the beach.

The world-class wave that broke on the island was what had first drawn Aidan to the area. Ten years ago it had held nothing but a poor, dilapidated village. Aidan had taken one look at that wave, seen the potential and known he'd have done anything to put a resort on it. And it had paid off. The island was one of the most profitable in the whole of the Fijian archipelago.

Spying the beach the surfers used to paddle out from he saw a flash of bright pink and caught the sweet sound of feminine laughter. Tensing he stopped and saw Cara in nothing but a gold bikini standing beside a surfer who was waxing his board. Her hands were on her hips and her body—that marvellous body—was being eaten up so much by the surfer's eyes that he'd be waxing the sand next if he wasn't careful.

Finally appeased to find an outlet for his agitation Aidan told Ben he'd catch up with him later and stalked towards the unsuspecting couple.

As he drew closer he recognised the man as a top-notch surfing sensation and a top-notch womaniser.

Wondering why his gaze was riveted to Cara's middle Aidan glanced down and saw one of the sexiest tattoos he had ever seen. Circling Cara's belly button was a ring of— were they flowers? No, they were hearts. Tiny red hearts almost overlapping one another.

He swallowed and felt a rush of heat tighten his muscles. Dammit if that surfer wasn't imagining running his tongue around that sexy little tattoo of hers.

Containing his temper as best he could he wasn't at all mollified when Cara glanced at him warily.

The surfer nodded at him when Cara made the introductions but Aidan didn't return the gesture. Instead he stepped closer to Cara in a purely possessive move that was designed to let the other man know she was off-limits.

The man got the message and with the trace of a smile loped off towards the water.

'What have you been doing all morning?'

She looked at him quizzically. 'Caught up on emails. Finally texted Christos and my sister.'

'What did you tell them?'

'I took your advice and said nothing. I told them that I was fine and would explain everything later.'

She shifted her feet and sand flicked up over the edge of his shoes. They both glanced down and he felt like an idiot standing fully dressed beside a woman in a tiny bikini.

'As a general rule I don't mind what you get up to,' he began, 'but I would ask that you don't flirt with other men while you're here.'

'I wasn't flirting,' she defended. 'I was talking.'

'This is my resort, Cara, and to all intents and purposes you are here as my partner. Please conduct yourself as such.'

'I didn't know it was your resort. Why didn't you tell me?'

'It wasn't relevant.'

'Well, I wasn't flirting. Jon-Jon said he would give me a surfing lesson later on today.'

Like hell.

'It's too dangerous for you out there.'

'It looks fun. Maybe you should try it, too. You know, live dangerously. *Cut loose.*'

Her tone told him that she didn't think he had it in him and his ego rebelled. He knew how to *'cut loose'.*

He used to ride a Ducati and go heli-skiing in the Alps. Hell, he had even planned to participate in the treacherous Sydney to Hobart yacht race one year. No, he was just driven. *Focused.* There was a difference. Not that Cara would probably recognise it. She was so intent on having a good time.

'Sometimes there's more to life than having fun,' he shot at her.

'I know that.'

Her quiet pronouncement annoyed him. 'Do you?'

'Yes. In fact, I was thinking of finding you and asking

if you needed any help while we were here, but I'm not sure that's a good idea.'

'Help?' He couldn't stop his eyes from dropping to her bikini. 'Dressed like that?'

Because the only help he could think of her offering right now was the kind that came with them both naked and sweaty on his bed.

'Yes.' She shoved her hands on her hips and stared at him mutinously. 'In case it escaped your notice almost everyone on the island is dressed like this. Even some of your conference attendees are wearing shorts.'

Were they? He hadn't noticed.

'Why do you want to help?'

Some of her anger seemed to leave her at his question. 'I don't know…I like to keep busy. I can't stop thinking about that horrible bet.' She checked herself and smiled faintly. 'Plus, you helped me out yesterday and after I took your limousine I feel like I should do something to make up for it. With your PA having quit…oh, never mind. I can see by your face that you think it's a stupid idea.'

Unable to remember the last time a woman had offered to help him out, Aidan paused. Women usually approached him for a job in his office or a job in his bed.

Sometimes both.

They didn't just offer to do things for him whether they owed him something or not. It was just expected that because he had the monetary resources he would provide for them. Which he didn't mind. It was just that Cara Chatsfield of all people offering to help him out…

Again he wondered if he hadn't misjudged her and it wasn't easy to get his head around because, yes, part of him still harboured the belief that deep down she was just a grubby little socialite with a lofty sense of entitlement.

'What can you do?' he asked gruffly.

Her face immediately brightened. 'I could answer your phone for you while you're in sessions.'

'No one has this number unless they're important.'

'Okay, well, maybe I could check your emails and tell you if there's anything urgent.'

'The information in my emails is sensitive.'

'Oh, right. Well, do you need any typing done?'

He was curious. 'Can you type?'

'Of course.' She scrunched her nose. 'But if you mean fast, then…no.'

'Can you use Excel?'

'On second thought, forget I asked. There isn't anything I would be any use to you for so…I'll just sit on the beach.'

Aidan wasn't at all sure he wanted her sitting on a beach in that bikini without a chaperone.

'There is one thing you can do for me. I need someone to check the building of the school in the local village.' It wasn't true. He had a surveyor coming at some point who would carry out an independent assessment of the work done, but hell, there was only so long he could look at those long golden legs without wanting to wrap them around his hips. His very naked hips. 'Last year the school needed to be rebuilt because of flood damage. It's been a massive undertaking and I haven't had a chance to look it over to assess whether the work carried out was adequate. You could go down there, wander around and give me your impression of how it looks. Nothing formal, just…impressions.'

'Really?'

'You wanted something useful to do.'

'Yes!' She beamed a smile at him that made him feel instantly guilty. 'Yes, I did.'

He nodded. Cleared his throat before he spoke. 'Great. It should only take an hour. Lunch will be served on the main restaurant terrace at one o'clock.'

'I'll be there.'

He watched her head back to the bungalow until she was out of sight before turning towards the specially designed conference facilities. He couldn't quite get into his head that she was as genuine as she seemed. In his experience where there was smoke there was fire and she was a Chatsfield—one of Britain's most notorious families. And while her reputation didn't make her a bad person per se, it did confirm his view that women generally prioritised their own needs above and beyond anyone else's.

And two hours later she proved the rule.

'Are you sure she's coming, Aidan. I'm really looking forward to meeting her. She's so beautiful.'

Aidan unlocked his jaw long enough to answer Ben's charming wife, Kate. 'I believe she said she would come, but—' *she's probably off chatting up another surfer* '—I suspect she's lost track of time.'

He got up and stalked over to where Dinesh was seating conference attendees—the ones in shorts!

'Dinesh, have you seen my guest?'

'Ms Chatsfield. Yes, boss. I showed her where the school was earlier. She's a keeper, that one.'

No, Aidan wanted to correct him: she *needed* a keeper.

Irritated by the other man's assessment, he snapped, 'Hold off on serving our table lunch, will you. She's supposed to be here.'

Of course he could just leave her where she was and continue lunch without her. He didn't require her to be at the table. That didn't matter. She had agreed to meet him and he was a man who kept his word and expected others to do the same.

Cara was in heaven. It was market day in the island village and all the locals had their wares on display on cloth-covered tables. Having finished wandering around the primary school and noting down her observations Cara couldn't resist meandering amongst the tables with some of the schoolchildren trailing after her, chatting and holding her hand.

She couldn't wait to give Aidan her notes to show him that she was more than just a pretty face, which by his comments earlier was all he thought she was.

Smiling she picked up a gorgeous sarong.

Aidan had been right about her being able to lay low on the island. The locals had no clue who she was, or didn't care, and the other guests were busy relaxing or at the conference. Of course her problems hadn't magically disappeared in the warm tropical air—such a pity—but she had no intention of interrupting her good mood by thinking about the future right now.

'You like to buy one?'

An older, matronly woman with frizzy hair voiced the question and Cara found herself testing the quality of the fabric she held in her hand. It was excellent.

'Yes, actually.' She dipped into the small leather purse she wore diagonally across her body. The colour would perfectly match Cilla's eyes. 'The colour and texture of the fabric is really beautiful.'

'My daughter, Jenny, makes it herself.' The woman smiled proudly.

Cara smiled back. It surprised her how friendly everyone was. How much they liked to chat.

Especially if the topic was Prince Aidan. It seemed that the man could do no wrong in their eyes. And Cara had to admit that she was pretty impressed to find out that Aidan put 80 per cent of the profits made by the resort back into the village to provide for the locals. Apparently his view was that this was their island and they were bestowing him a gift by letting him share it with others. Something she hadn't expected from a billionaire businessman who had showed no remorse in trying to ruin Martin Ellery the other night. No remorse until the end, that was.

Without warning she remembered the flash of pain she had thought she'd seen in his eyes when he'd been talking about Martin Ellery and she wondered at it. She had been able to pick up that the animosity between the two men went back a long way but it was obviously a touchy subject because twice she had asked about it and twice she had been instantly closed down for her trouble. Not that she would have expected Aidan to open up to her because she was a stranger but still…she was a stranger he had kissed. A stranger he had touched.

Feeling a now-familiar ache low down in her body whenever she remembered how it felt to be in his arms Cara tamped down on her thoughts. Being attracted to Aidan Kelly only proved her sister's theory that she really was attracted to men who were only interested in short-term liaisons.

Better to think of him as a friend—if even that—and forget all about how stupidly gorgeous he was. He wasn't for her and she'd promised herself a year ago that once she found out a guy wasn't right for her, then she'd move on.

And really, she should be glad nothing was going to happen between them because her life was too messed up right now to complicate it even more by imagining that this fake relationship was even a real friendship.

It wasn't.

They were two people who had met by chance and who would be going their separate ways after tomorrow. And she couldn't have been happier. It would be one less person judging her and finding her lacking in some way.

Realising that the older woman was still chatting, and

that she had completely lost the thread of the conversation, Cara tuned back in.

'Jenny also works with the Fijian black pearls. Would you like to see them?'

'I'd love to.'

The woman reached beneath the table and pulled out a large beat-up metal box. When she opened it Cara's breath caught. Inside, laid out in velvet-lined sections, were clusters of pearls of all sizes and colours ranging from the deepest black to gunmetal grey and an amber brown that defied description. Most of them were delicately strung together with the finest leather strips that were a perfect foil for the shiny pearls.

'Oh, my gosh, these are amazing. Can I touch them?'

'Of course. I not put them out yet until Jenny arrives.'

Cara reached into the box and pulled out a bracelet of three pearls strung side by side and separated by tiny knots in the fine leather cord. The jeweller had twisted sections of the leather in such a way that it didn't detract from the centrepiece. The effect was effortless and visually stunning.

This was what Cara loved to do. Find quirky combinations of clothes and jewellery and make them work together. She had often thought about opening a shop at some stage in the future that combined high-street wear with vintage pieces in the one place. Now, studying the beautiful Fijian colours and designs, she wondered if it were at all possible to open a shop that offered an array of both clothing and jewellery from different cultures all in one place. She thought about her own favourite pieces. Scarves from Paris, slippers and shawls from Nepal, her Aztec earrings, her Texan cowboy boots.

A vision started to unfold in her mind.

'Does Jenny sell these on the international market?'

'Oh, no. She just finish her schooling in Australia thanks to Mr Kelly and—oh, here he is.'

Cara glanced over her shoulder to see Aidan Kelly bearing down on them and he didn't look happy.

'Mr Kelly. *Bula.*'

'*Bula*, Esther, how are you?'

'Better than you.' The older woman laughed, presenting her cheek for him to kiss. 'You look hot and busy. Need to slow down, Mr Kelly.'

'So you say every time I visit.'

'Still the same, though.' The old woman gave a theatrical sigh. 'You the only person I know who never get into Fijian time.'

'Fijian time?' Cara said.

'The locals here move at a pace all of their own making,' Aidan said with a brief smile. 'We, in Australia, call it slow.'

'It's what people come here for. To chill out. Relax. Life meant to be enjoyed,' Esther informed him.

Aidan's searing gaze latched on to Cara's. 'Some people do that better than others. Haven't you forgotten something?'

'What— Oh, my God. You invited me to lunch.'

'Which was due to start twenty minutes ago.'

'Oh, I'm so sorry.' Cara handed back the beautiful pearl bracelet. 'Thank you, Esther. Tell your daughter I think she's a genius.'

Esther leaned closer and laid her hand on Cara's arm. 'Men never like women shopping. He will be okay.'

Cara wasn't so sure and she had to stretch her legs to keep up with Aidan as he strode across the soft sand, completely ignoring the crystal-clear water that lapped onto the shoreline. She felt terrible for keeping him waiting and knew that, once again, she had mucked up.

'I'm sorry I—'

His grim expression stayed her. The light banter around the word they had shared the night before was nowhere in sight. 'You weren't going to say that again.'

'Except I seem to keep messing up with you and I can see you're really upset.'

'I expect people to keep to their obligations when they make them. Clearly shopping was more important than keeping to yours.'

Aidan saw her flinch as if he had slapped her and it made him want to find the nearest boxing ring. Maybe Dinesh would do a few rounds with him later on to help him work off some of his pent-up energy.

Knowing that on some level his reaction was over the top Aidan stalked off and absently listened to the squeak of their feet on the sand. When Cara remained silent beside him he realised that she had retreated inside herself and his frustration with the whole situation grew.

Stopping, he pulled her into the shade of a palm tree— the slow, rhythmical swish of the ocean behind him almost mocking his foul mood. 'Dammit, why are you letting me push you around like this?'

She wouldn't meet his eyes. 'Because you want to think the worst of me and you're right, saying that I lost track of time is just lame.'

'But it happens,' he excused, wondering what had happened to the rational side of his brain.

She gave a glum smile. 'It doesn't happen to you.'

He thought of his performance earlier at the conference, or rather his non-performance. He wanted to tell her that he wasn't sure what was happening to him, but...

She swallowed and his eyes dropped to the creamy column of her throat and lower to the brightly coloured sarong she had tied over her breasts. It hid everything and nothing, the carelessly tied centre knot making his fingers itch to tug it loose.

The warm breeze stirred the straight edges of her short hair. 'What have you done to your hair now?'

She reached up at his unexpected question and fingered the row of tiny plaits. 'A couple of the schoolgirls put a few braids through it while I wrote up my notes about the school. Here they are, by the way.'

Aidan took the two neatly folded pieces of notepaper and stuffed them into his pocket. How could he be angry with her when all she'd been doing was taking the time to be friendly with the islanders?

Well, he'd expected her to be lying on the beach entertaining some randy surfer, that was why.

He shook his head. He had to get a grip. For some reason Cara reminded him of his mother. Or rather, she reminded him of how it felt when his mother had left. Hollow and...sad. Emotions that were debilitating and destructive. Emotions he never wanted to experience again after seeing how badly they had affected his father.

Looking down at her he wondered what it was about her that made him remember all that. Wondered what it was about her that made him want to reach out and run his hand down the smooth skin of her cheek. Made him want to ignore all logic and just sink into her welcoming body until he couldn't think of anything at all.

'Aidan?'

Her soft query brought his eyes back to her lustrous grey ones. He frowned and she glanced away from him.

Grey?

'Look at me?'

She did, but he might as well have been a headmaster holding out a metre-long cane.

Wanting to shake off the heavy vibe, Aidan sucked in a deep breath and realised she was right about him wanting to think the worst of her. The chemistry between them was so red-hot he needed every excuse he could come up with to keep from acting on it.

Remembering her comment from the day before about channelling some movie star, he instinctively knew that her eye colour wasn't natural. 'Who are you channelling today?'

'Aishwarya Rai.'

'Who?'

'A really talented Indian actress with the most incredible eyes.'

Aidan shook his head. 'What's wrong with just being yourself, Cara?'

She sifted a layer of silky white sand between red-painted toenails. 'Oh, you don't want me to do that. I'm boring.'

Yeah, about as boring as a Cirque du Soleil show. But he could see she believed it and he wanted to press her up against the trunk of the palm tree and show her just how boring she wasn't.

As if somehow reading his mind, she made to move past him but her movements were jerky and uncoordinated and she stumbled. Aidan reached for her, his hands sliding around her torso, his thumbs pressing into the slight swell of her small breasts.

Lust, hot and powerful, punched him in the gut and he revelled in the feel of her lithe frame between his large hands. He was almost a head taller than her and she had to tilt her head back to look up at him. The movement exposed the long line of her throat and the deep V of her cleavage where the tight sarong pulled her breasts together.

Her hands gripped his biceps and the pulse point in the base of her throat beat at a rapid pace that matched his own.

Her heat enveloped him, her scent consumed him, and Aidan wanted to kiss her so badly in that moment he didn't even realise that one hand had moved to the back of her head until the ferry that visited the island twice a day let out three sharp whistles.

It was enough to break whatever spell he was under and Aidan pulled back, shocked at how close he'd come to giving in to the impulse to kiss her.

This was crazy.

Already he was thinking about her too much and he didn't like it. He didn't like anything he couldn't categorise and she was defying every box he tried to fit her into. Until he worked her out, until… Hell.

Until nothing.

He stepped back. Ran his hand through his hair. Righted his breathing. 'How long will it take you to change for lunch?'

Surprise registered on her face. 'You still want me to come to lunch?'

Telling himself that he was completely in control, Aidan checked his watch. 'Have you eaten?'

'No, but—'

'Then how long?'

CHAPTER TEN

'WHY PINK?' KATE, the woman Cara had struck up an instant rapport with over lunch, leaned across the outdoor dining table with a huge smile on her face and drew her attention away from the view of the azure-blue water and the picture-perfect islands in the distance. The sense of space gave the outdoor restaurant a calm ambience despite how busy it was. Cara had just been thinking about how she felt about the call she had received from her agent on the walk to the restaurant. It seemed that it wasn't only Christos who was impressed by her newfound relationship with the esteemed Aidan Kelly; the Demarche deal was back on the table. Or a variation of the deal.

'Basically,' Harriet had said, 'it's between you and America's latest sweetheart. You both turn up at the gala dinner next Sunday night, strut your stuff, and they'll make a decision on the night.'

Sort of like a test, Cara thought, knowing that they were probably hedging their bets with her in case something else went wrong between now and then.

Cara's first thought was that she was insulted by the idea of parading around a room full of people while corporate executives sat back and rated her. But then she reminded herself that modelling was competitive and if she wanted the deal, then she'd have to forsake her pride and just do it. And what could go wrong between now and then? She was on a tropical island with a respected businessman. A respected businessman she felt drawn to like a moth to a flame.

Thankfully, he seemed to have more sense than her and she had joked with him on the way to the restaurant that at least one of them was faring well in the reputation stakes out of their pretend union, but the truth was, she didn't want to have a negative impact on Aidan.

The realisation had given her pause because no matter how hard she tried to pretend that he was just another man who would pass through her life, a part of her knew that wasn't true.

A part of her knew that if they had made love the other night it would have been unforgettable. That he would have been unforgettable. Which was a problem because life had taught Cara that she was infinitely forgettable to those she cared about the most.

A splash sounded in the nearby infinity pool and Cara returned her attention to Kate.

'I mean, I love it on you,' Kate continued, 'but I don't think I'd ever be game to do it myself.'

'It was a spur-of-the-moment thing,' Cara admitted. Like most things in her life, she mused, completely unplanned.

'Sometimes they're the best decisions. And—' Kate leaned her elbows on the linen tablecloth '—speaking of spur-of-the-moment things, I'm dying to know how you and Aidan met.'

Cara felt her mouth open and close as her mind whirred for something to say. 'I…' Foolishly she hadn't expected anyone to ask her this kind of question on the island and she was completely unprepared.

'Oh, I've embarrassed you.' Kate grimaced. 'Please

don't mind my brashness. I'm the mother of a toddler—
my life is officially boring.'

From what Cara had seen of Kate and Ben's love for
their daughter earlier she very much doubted that. But who
was she to judge? Her own mother had obviously found
motherhood a trial.

'You don't like being a mother?'

Kate looked startled. 'No. I mean, yes.' She laughed.
'I've given you the wrong impression. I *love* being a
mother. No, I'm just so curious. I've never seen Aidan so
off-stride and I think you and I are going to be firm friends
in the future.' She lowered her voice. 'Did you really meet
when Aidan bet on you in a poker game?' She shivered. 'I
know the papers played it up as sordid, but secretly I found
the whole thing terribly romantic.'

If only, Cara thought. Then she remembered Aidan's
earlier reaction about her behaving as his 'partner' for the
time she was on the island and Cara wondered if he would
want her to pretend that their relationship was something
it wasn't to Kate.

On some level it felt wrong to lie, and yet if she told
Kate the truth she would know that all the times Aidan had
refilled her water glass for her over lunch without asking
and ordered her coffee just the way she liked it while she
had been in the bathroom had been nothing but a sham.

Glancing over at Aidan deep in conversation with a
small group of men she was instantly taken by how tall
and sexy he was in another superbly cut suit, his strong
thighs and wide shoulders accentuated rather than dimin-
ished by his clothing. She had a brief moment of wondering what he would look like naked and her breath caught.
Would he have hair on his chest, or not? Would his ab-
dominal muscles really be as defined as they had felt the
other night on the sofa?

The almost-kiss they'd shared outside jumped to the front of her mind. The way he'd looked at her. For a moment she had sensed that he had wanted her as much as she wanted him and the realisation had made her want to throw caution to the wind and forget that their values weren't aligned. Forget that he would never want her after he'd slept with her.

As if sensing her gaze he glanced over at her and raised his chin ever so slightly as if asking if she was okay. She knew her face had flushed as if she'd just been caught with her hand in the silver drawer and she ducked her head, deciding that she would keep her story to Kate as close to the truth as she could.

'No, we didn't actually *meet* then,' she informed Kate slowly. 'We sort of met when we ran into each other at the airport.'

Kate leaned her elbows on the table. 'Do tell.'

'It's not that exciting. I was trying to find my phone in my bag and stepped into Aidan's path and then my shoe broke.'

'And he stopped to help you.'

'Yes. We, ah, talked.' *He thought I was a hooker. I thought he was horrible.* 'And then he gave me a lift into town.' *Kind of.* 'And it just sort of went from there….' *And please don't ask me about the time frame because then you'll know this is all just a ruse.*

But Kate didn't ask. She just sat back in the teak dining chair and sighed. 'It sounds very romantic. Ben and I met by chance, as well. He was a guest lecturer at the university I was studying at and I had decided not to go to the lecture—imagining that this corporate ass was coming to patronise the little people—and at the last minute I turned up. It was love at first sight for us, too.'

'Oh, it's not love at first sight for Aidan and me,' Cara sputtered.

Kate touched her hand. 'It's obvious you're both completely smitten. You can't keep your eyes off each other.'

Embarrassed that she had been caught out, and sure that Kate was referring to her more than Aidan, she smiled gratefully as Kate's toddler wandered over and nearly stuck ice-cream-covered hands all over Kate's designer skirt.

Before Cara could warn her about the impending disaster Kate grabbed the child's hands and held them aloft as she tickled her daughter with her other hand. 'You little rascal. Go do that to Daddy.'

'Daddy work.'

'Yes.' Kate threw Cara a conspiratorial glance. 'Go to Uncle Aidan. He's always got time for his goddaughter's sticky hands. Go and show him.'

Kate gave Cara an impish grin as they watched the tiny girl in a pink-spotted dress toddle up to Aidan and tug on his jacket.

Cara was mesmerised, wondering how he would react, watching avidly as he glanced down and automatically scooped the little girl into his arms, completely oblivious to the disaster being rendered on his jacket. When Ben nudged him, Aidan glanced down at the creamy smear near his shoulder. Ben grabbed a napkin from a nearby table and wiped the little girl's hands and Cara's heart jumped against her ribs when both men grinned instead of growing angry.

And from there it was impossible to prevent herself from imagining what it would be like to have a child with a man like that. What it would feel like if they were a real couple. She was very much afraid it would feel a lot like love. For her, anyway...

And who's to say it couldn't be? she thought.

Love happened when you least expected it, didn't it? Why was she so certain that it could never happen for her?

The little girl had the same caramel-coloured hair as Aidan and could almost be his daughter. She heard Kate giggle beside her and glanced at Ben just in time to catch the look of retribution he threw at his wife.

Cara didn't even try to hold in her smile. Now *that* was true love, she thought, unable to swallow past the lump in her throat.

She watched as Emma squirmed out of Aidan's arms and then rushed back to throw herself at her mother. Kate scooped her up and landed kisses all over her soft cheeks.

For Cara family didn't involve parents. It involved only her adored siblings. It had been Lucilla and Antonio who had changed her nappies and fed her when her constant crying had sent another nanny running to a different job. It had been Orsino who had put Band-Aids on her elbows and knees when she'd tried to follow the twins up the side of Chatsfield House in a game of cops and robbers. It had been Lucca who had helped her through her art courses. It had been Nicolo who had pulled the cigarette from her fourteen-year-old lips after she'd returned home from boarding school and told her he'd beat her senseless if he ever caught her smoking again. And it had been Franco who taught her how to avoid the media—not that she'd learned that lesson very well.

In her deepest, most cherished dreams, though, this was what a real family looked like. A man and a woman who loved each other enough to push through any bad times, and a child they adored beyond comprehension.

The four Fijian guitarists entertaining the dwindling lunch crowd out on the wide deck were superb. Aidan folded his arms as Emma reached up to take Cara's hands so she could spin her in yet another dizzy circle on the dance floor.

'She's nice,' Ben commented. 'Different from what I thought she would be, though don't hit me for saying that.'

Aidan glanced at Ben. 'Why would I hit you for saying that?'

Ben shrugged. 'I'd clock any man I thought was making a derogatory comment about Kate.'

Aidan didn't want to reply to that because it had been his first reaction, as well.

He wondered what Ben would think if he told him how Cara had commandeered his car and allowed herself to be used as a stake in a game of poker. Then he realised that he no longer cared about all that.

Instead he had been contemplating how she had struck up an easy rapport with the islanders and even had the schoolchildren braiding her hair. It was true that the islanders were incredibly friendly, but most were quite shy, and didn't easily permit intimacies such as touching. That thought brought to mind the look they had shared after lunch. The soft glow of her face had reminded him of how beautifully flushed she had been in his arms the other night. How her flesh had leaped at his touch with a hunger that seemed to match his own. And then outside earlier, when he'd nearly given in to temptation once again in full view of anyone walking past.

Hell.

He swiped a hand through his hair and acknowledged that his current edginess was as much from sexual frustration as anything else.

Watching her dancing wasn't doing anything to improve things, either, and he turned his back on her and stuck his hand in his pocket.

His hand came into contact with the carefully handwritten notes she'd made about the school building and he pulled them out. He'd pocketed them with just a cursory glance before and he felt a little guilty now. Sending her on a fool's mission hadn't been his finest moment and he hadn't expected her to put any real effort into the task.

As if reading his mind Ben interrupted his thoughts. 'Kate said that you sent Cara to check out the school earlier, but you do know we have a surveyor coming next week, right?'

'Yeah, I know,' Aidan replied. 'I was just giving her something to do to keep her out of the way.'

Unfortunately the guitarists chose that moment to end their set and Aidan heard a small gasp behind him and knew instantly who it was and that she had heard him.

He turned slowly and felt like the lowest life form on earth as Cara quickly tried to mask her hurt expression.

'Excuse me, I have to…' Her voice trailed off and she spun around and walked quickly across the terrace.

Ben pulled a sympathetic face. 'You're in the doghouse tonight, my friend.'

Which would probably be the best place for him, Aidan acknowledged silently, that way he wouldn't be tempted to do something his instinct warned him away from every time he saw her.

Hell.

As she disappeared around a clump of dark green rubber plants that separated the beach from the resort path he heaved a massive sigh that spoke volumes of his inner turmoil.

Part of him wanted to rush after her while another, more saner part warned him to back off. Warned him that he wasn't himself right now and that it would be better to put some distance between them. That running after her now would send her entirely the wrong message. That it might make her feel more important than she was.

Even so, he'd already taken a step in her direction; the urge to follow her was that strong. The realisation stopped him and his vacillation was testament to the battle raging inside of him. He didn't want to want to go after her. He didn't want to want her this much at all. He wanted order back in his life.

Neatness.

Purpose.

And the girl with the pink hair and long legs would not bring that. She'd bring passion, disorder, *emotion*—all things that were a sign of weakness. And try as he might he couldn't find a logical reason for the all-consuming lust he felt for her.

That's because there isn't one.

Or was there?

He'd made her forbidden fruit, hadn't he? Off-limits. He'd always been a person who thrived on challenges and he'd damned well challenged himself when he'd decided to ignore what lay between them as thick and annoying as mosquitos at a lake on a summer's day.

Tell a person not to think of a pink elephant and what did they do? Think of a pink elephant. Tell a man he couldn't sleep with a desirable woman with pink hair and a face like a goddess and what did he want…?

Aidan grinned. Relief flooded him and he blew out a long breath. He felt settled again. Lighter. He eased his shoulders away from his ears. No crick. His grin widened. Finally, he felt like himself again. Back in control.

One more day and then vamoose; she'd return to her world and he'd return to his. For Aidan, restoring balance back into his life couldn't come quickly enough.

CHAPTER ELEVEN

'WHY ARE YOU PACKING?'

Cara threw her nightie into her case and sniffed back the angry tears that threatened to spill over. She hadn't heard Aidan come in and she'd like to pretend that he still hadn't. But she was done with crying in front of him. Done with crying because yet another man found her lacking.

Of all the times she'd been rejected in her life it shocked her to realise that this one somehow hurt the most. Probably because she'd been having such a nice time at lunch and Aidan had once again lulled her with his kind gestures towards her.

Acting, she thought flatly, *for his friends*.

Stupid. She'd let her guard down with him. Again! For a moment she had even *liked* him. Well, she corrected herself, she had liked his body. Because how could it be anything else when he was still the arrogant man who had tried to give her fifty dollars for her broken shoe at the airport? The same man who had demanded she strip for him in his hotel room and then who had held her so tenderly. Had kissed her so—

Enough.

No more thinking about kissing Aidan Kelly. It had left her looking like a fool more than once.

And she should be glad she'd found out how little he regarded her before anything more happened between them because, while it might be scorching hot, it would only be temporary and would no doubt end in heartache. Her heartache.

What she should have done was stick to her original plan to hide out at her agent's house in L.A. Not that Aidan had given her much of a choice, but dammit, he was right; she had to stop letting him push her around. And she would this time.

Not that he would probably try and stop her from leaving. He'd probably be glad to see the back of her. That would explain his inconsistent behaviour towards her. He didn't really want her around.

'I was just giving her something to do to keep her out of the way.'

He and Christos both. He and her father. Not that her father had ever given her something to do. Rather he just sent her to boarding school and then left her at the Chatsfield House with the servants during holidays.

Oh, her siblings had been there over the years, but they had been a lot older and they'd had their own lives to lead and Cara hadn't wanted to bother them with her concerns and feelings of inadequacy. That should have been her mother's role.

She thought about Kate and her small daughter over lunch. The way Kate had scooped Emma up in her arms and smooched the little girl's neck until she'd collapsed into peals of laughter.

Tears formed behind Cara's eyes and she wondered where her mother was right now. What she was doing. She had been relatively young when she had walked out on Cara and her siblings. Did she have another family now? Another child she had adored more than her?

'I asked you a question.'

Aidan's gruff interruption thankfully wrecked her train of thought and she hardened her heart and kept packing. 'Go away.'

She felt like she was made of wood. Aidan didn't want her. He didn't even like her. His lack of respect when he'd spoken to Ben had been palpable. 'I'm going home.'

'You said that was the worst place for you.'

'Well, now I've decided that here is.'

'I'm sorry I hurt you.'

She shrugged and sniffed. 'I'm surprised you noticed.'

'I noticed.'

Cara didn't respond to that. It didn't mean anything. Even a blind insect would have noticed her distress. 'Congratulations.'

'Cara, I'd like you to stay.'

Surprised by the sincerity in his voice, Cara turned towards him. He had his hands deep in his pockets and he looked…pensive.

'Why?'

'I promised you a couple of days respite and I feel like you haven't really had that.'

'And you always keep your promises.'

It wasn't a question but he answered it anyway. 'Yes.'

She shook her head. 'You made me feel horrible. Even worse than Christos did. At least I expected it from him.'

'I'm sorry.'

'That word is becoming overused between us.'

'Yes.' He shifted uncomfortably. 'I hadn't thought about how to deal with questions about you.'

'You hadn't! How do you think I felt?' Cara cried. 'I spent a good amount of time convincing Kate—who I really like, by the way—that this was real between us. She's going to think I'm either a terrible liar or completely deluded.'

'Why did you do that?'

'Because earlier you told me to conduct myself as your partner and… It doesn't matter.'

She felt stupid.

Confounded at having found her half packed, Aidan was at a loss. 'I didn't mean what I said to Ben.' Cara wouldn't look at him and Aidan took a deep breath. 'What I said was inconsiderate.'

'But true.'

Aidan closed his eyes. 'If you must know I sent you to the school because I didn't want you sitting around on the beach all day by yourself.' Especially after he'd seen that sexy tattoo that should have been for his eyes only.

She looked over at him, her grey eyes shiny with unshed tears. 'What could possibly go wrong with me sitting on a beach? You said yourself that there were no paparazzi and—'

'It wasn't that.' He gritted his teeth. 'I saw you in that bikini and I knew I'd never concentrate while I imagined every surfer on the island trying to come on to you.'

'Why wouldn't you concentrate?'

Aidan thought about answering that truthfully. Thought about admitting that she had somehow gotten under his skin and that every time he was in spitting distance of her it was all he could do not to touch her.

He thought about telling her that for about five seconds and then he went for the other answer. The safe one. Because why open a tin of worms when he wasn't sure yet what he would find inside?

'You're my guest and therefore my responsibility,' he said obliquely.

Her eyes met his briefly and then she turned back to the cases on the bed and kept packing.

Aidan felt like throwing his hands in the air. What had she expected him to say? That he wanted to protect her? Wanted to look after her? That he was *jealous*? 'Look, I'm not myself right now,' he growled.

'Why not?'

He took a deep breath. 'I don't want to get into it but—'

'Is it Martin Ellery? I heard Ben mention him over lunch and you didn't look the same from then on.'

Aidan felt dull colour leach into his face. He thought he'd hidden his reaction to the news that Martin Ellery was making noises about fighting him for the TV rights to the AFL—the biggest TV contract in Australia and the one jewel in his father's crown that Ellery hadn't snatched away fourteen years ago.

'Ellery doesn't matter,' he said curtly.

Blatantly disbelieving him, if the look on her face was anything to go by, she turned away again and this time Aidan did throw his hands in the air. Dammit, couldn't she see that he was trying here?

He took a calming breath as she zipped her largest suitcase and tried another tack. It was either that or shove the cases off the bed and lay her on it. Somehow, he thought in a moment of black humour, he didn't think she'd be too receptive to that.

'I read the notes you took on the school.'

She paused before zipping a smaller case. 'Please, I don't want to know what you think.'

Unable to stand by and watch her leave he gripped her shoulders and spun her towards him. 'They're good.'

She shrugged him off and moved to the window. 'You don't have to say that. I know you planned to send a professional out.'

'I don't say things I don't mean. Not only did you notice that the manager had skimped on the teacher's quarters but you picked up the fact that the children need more art supplies and updated books. And yes, I was planning to send in a surveyor—and I still will for the structural soundness of the building—but he wouldn't have picked up on all the areas the manager had tried to cut back on.'

Her brows drew together. 'Why would he try to cut back on a school? That's detrimental to the kids.'

'He's ambitious and he was trying to bring the whole thing in under budget to impress me.'

She pulled a face. 'That makes sense, I suppose.'

'Not on a community project. But he's learned his lesson now and won't do it again.'

'You sacked him?'

'No,' Aidan retorted, somewhat put out by her ready assessment that he would fire someone without giving them a second chance.

'I explained that while I expect the resort to be profitable I don't expect people to suffer to make it that way.'

'Oh. That's…nice.'

'I'm not an ogre, Cara.' So why did he feel like one right now? 'Please stay.'

She wrapped her arms around her torso as if she were cold. 'I don't know. I don't think that's a good idea.' She glanced towards the sparkling ocean beyond her window. 'I don't know what I want right now.'

Aidan took a step towards her. 'You can have whatever you want.'

She turned back to him and the vulnerable expression on her face stayed him. 'Maybe in your world, Aidan, but not in mine. I nearly lost a contract because of what happened last weekend. I still might. People are always judging me and finding me inadequate and the fact is that they're right. My own mother couldn't even stand me.'

Aidan heard the lost note in her voice and his brow furrowed. 'She said that?'

'Not directly. The only time I can ever remember hearing my mother's voice is on a video recording.'

'A video recording?'

'Gee, you really don't read the gossip columns, do you? She left when I was a baby.'

Realising that this was an incredibly sensitive area for her, he tread carefully. 'Why?'

'I was difficult.'

His brow drew together. 'As far as I know, mothers don't usually leave their babies because they're difficult.'

'I was horrible.' Her hands around her waist bunched the fabric of her T-shirt. 'I cried all the time. I wouldn't sleep. Apparently I was terrible at taking solids....'

Aidan recalled some of the press around the time her parents had separated. He'd been a lot younger so it was hazy but he remembered their break-up had been shrouded with talk of alcohol and women and bad business deals. None of which was Cara's fault. 'You can't seriously blame yourself for her leaving.'

'No. I know she had postnatal depression. I know her and my father were having troubles.'

Aidan moved beside her as her very real distress pierced deep inside him. 'Cara, you didn't make her leave.'

'I just said I know that.' She threw her hands up between them as if to ward him off. 'She wanted a different life and I wouldn't have fit into that. It's fine.'

Like hell it's fine. He reached out and gently drew her chin around so that she was looking at him. 'You didn't make her leave, Cara.'

She batted his hand away and crossed the room. 'You don't know that. If I'd been better, if I'd been prettier...'

'If you'd been smarter, or stronger. If the world had been

square…' He watched myriad emotions chase themselves across her face. Pain, despair, loss…*hope*? 'It's not logical, Cara. Your mother was an adult with six other children. No one knows why she left but her.'

'Well, if it wasn't me, then why couldn't my father stand me, either?' she asked challengingly. 'Why could he never look at me? Oh, I know the answer to that. Because I look like her and he hated that she left.'

Aidan thought about the ways she turned in on herself when she was really hurt. The way she revamped her image every now and then. It was an attempt to hide, he realised, a way of protecting the little girl who had grown up with selfish parents.

'I loved him,' she said almost too quietly for Aidan to hear. 'I still love him.'

It took Aidan two strides to reach her and then he stopped thinking and drew her into his arms. She stiffened for a heartbeat and then buried her face against his neck. 'I wasn't going to cry any more.'

'It's okay, sweetheart. You're okay.'

A broken sob caught in her throat and Aidan reached down and kissed her. It was the most natural thing in the world to do. 'You're okay,' he murmured gently.

The kiss was soft. Tender. And he steadfastly ignored the way holding her made his heart clench inside his chest. This was about her, not him.

You're okay. You're okay. You're okay.

Aidan's soft words went round and round inside Cara's head like an out-of-control merry-go-round picking up speed.

A horrible ball of mixed emotions grew inside her and threatened to engulf her. She felt sick. Unsteady. The urge to pull out of his embrace making her feel like she had live ants crawling all over her skin.

Inadvertently Aidan had hit on her worst fear. The fear that once someone looked inside of her, once someone saw the real her, they would find nothing worth keeping. Nothing worth loving. She had discovered that changing her looks and pretending she didn't care what others thought was easier. Easier to cope with her parents' rejection. And how Aidan was holding her. Kissing her. Making her feel special. Making her feel wanted. Her stomach twisted painfully. She couldn't stand his touch because it made her want things she knew she couldn't ever let herself want.

'Aidan?' Cara said his name shakily and placed her hands on his chest. 'Stop, please.'

Slowly he raised his head and stared down at her.

Cara held perfectly still, afraid that if she moved she might actually break.

'I know what I should do,' he said huskily, 'and I know what I want to do. They're two entirely different things.'

His raw admission made her pulse quicken and her face feel hot. She experienced the same heady rush of emotion she did on a roller-coaster and it was as if she was back on one now and about to go over. She could see the crashlanding below, but, oh, the soft press of his mouth… The hard press of his body… She knew he would be the type of lover who cared about his partner and just once she'd like to experience what it would be like to be with a man like that. Just once she'd like to experience what real chemistry felt like.

Only she knew it was a chemistry that he didn't want to feel and some deep instinct told her that this man had the potential to truly hurt her as she had never been before. That already she had made him more important than she should have and that right now she wasn't in control of herself enough not to make the physical attraction between them more than it actually was.

The last man she had been intimate with had ripped the stuffing out of her when he'd told her that she was too needy and she could feel those same feelings rising up inside her again. Those same feelings times one hundred.

She'd imagined herself in love with her last boyfriend but he had walked away and she hadn't thought about him since. She suspected if she went any further with Aidan, she'd think about him for ever.

The knowledge gave her the strength to push against him. 'I'm sorry, Aidan, please don't...'

As the words left her mouth she knew that she was so weak in the face of the desire he incited in her that if he pushed it, if he leaned down and kissed her again, she wouldn't stop him. She'd reach up and pull his head down to hers and forget all about the consequences and face them when they inevitably occurred as she faced down every other disaster in her life.

Only he didn't push it. He took a deep breath and released her before turning on his heel and walking away.

She didn't think she'd ever felt worse.

CHAPTER TWELVE

THE CONFERENCE WAS OVER. All that was left to do was to organise his jet to make ready to fly him home. For some reason Aidan hadn't done that, even though he knew Ellery had planned to meet with the AFL board this week. Of course he wouldn't be successful in his bid to win the contract, but even so, Aidan had sent Ben back to Sydney already to get a read on the situation.

He should have taken everything Ellery had when he'd had the chance and he still didn't have a handle on why he hadn't. The old restlessness that had been with him more and more lately was back and he felt like he was trudging through a swamp as he made his way back to the bungalow.

Would Cara still be there?

After she had pushed him away yesterday afternoon he hadn't seen her. Last night she'd claimed to have had a headache and couldn't accompany him to the conference dinner. This morning she'd still been in bed when he'd left.

Sometime during the closing session he'd come up with the crazy notion of taking Cara home with him to Sydney but then sanity had prevailed and he'd discounted that. Now, if she was still here, he'd offer her the chance to stay on another few days.

He knew she didn't have to be back in London until the end of the week, and given that she had to stay out of trouble to win the contract she seemed to desperately want, this was the best place for her.

Here, or with him.

A top-of-the-line sailboat caught his eye and he tried to recall the last time he'd been out on one. A memory stirred of him and three university mates pooling their resources and hiring a cabin cruiser for an hour around Sydney Harbour to impress their respective dates. Hell, had it really been that long? No. He'd been out on his corporate yacht many times since then. All on business…all entertaining key clients and political figures.

The cruiser he'd hired with his mates had been about fun. They'd laughed, drank beer, hell, he'd even danced! He shook his head. No one would expect him to do that now. Now he was a man who wore suits on a tropical island and allowed himself ten minutes for dinner if he wasn't entertaining a colleague or a woman as a precursor to sex.

When had his life evolved to this round robin of preordained events? And was that healthy? It was one thing to have focus, quite another to be obsessed with that focus. Automatically his mind fell to Martin Ellery and the thirst for revenge he had carried around inside of himself for so long. Cara's words about forgiveness came back to haunt him. Would she have carried around a bag of hate inside her heart as big as a hot-air balloon as he had? Would she have gone after Martin Ellery with the precise determination to ruin his life? Would she have made it her primary goal to be bigger, better and stronger than someone else just to beat them? He doubted it.

But *he* had. He'd pursued Ellery because it gave him a higher purpose.

Yeah, some higher purpose that was. God, he could be a sanctimonious bastard when he wanted to be.

An image of Cara at the lunch table came into his mind. She was a graceful and natural hostess and it was clear she liked people. *Accepted* people for who they were despite the deep scars he sensed had been left behind by the combined abandonment of her parents. Picturing her as a young girl craving a morsel of her father's affection made something heavy settle behind his chest. Something that made his hands clench tight. He hated to think that she had been hurt, that she was still hurt....

She was soft, he knew that now. Too soft, in some ways. And she was looking for love. For what Ben and Kate shared. But Ben and Kate were the exception, not the rule. And Aidan had seen firsthand what happened to a man when he chose love and it went wrong. It blinded him. *Weakened* him.

He stopped just as he reached the end of the path leading to their private bungalow. Cara was leaning on the deck and staring out at the ocean. Aidan's eyes followed her line of vision and he saw a row of surfers in the lineup for the incoming waves.

It was an epic day. The waves were big and clean and sucking out into perfectly formed barrels. His palms itched to get out there. To cast his concerns aside for a moment and just *be*.

His eyes returned to Cara. She had on a bright T-shirt and a pair of lightweight trousers. Travel clothes.

A hoot went up in the water and he turned back to see a silhouette bottom turn into a perfect tube and suddenly his feet were carrying him swiftly up the steps to the bungalow.

Cut loose, she'd challenged him. He'd show her cutting loose!

Startled by his sudden appearance, Cara turned and gripped her hands together. 'I've packed and—'

'We're not leaving right away.'

'We're not?'

'No. I thought I might catch a few waves first.'

'You surf?' The look of surprise on her face almost made him laugh and he felt lighter than he had in days.

'Sweetheart, I used to compete.'

Well, locally anyway, but she didn't need to know that.

An hour later Aidan felt invigorated and alive, the blood pumping through his veins and the water streaming off his back as he pulled his board out of the shallows and headed onto the beach.

He knew exactly where Cara was. Hell, all the guys did. With her pink hair and gold-bikini-clad body standing on the edge of the shore she'd managed to distract the others enough that Aidan had caught some ripping waves—and missed some others when she'd stretched her hands over her head and waved when she had spotted him.

With adrenaline surging through his veins he loped towards her.

She scowled up at him, her hands on her waist, her legs apart. She looked like a veritable fishwife only so absolutely stunning a man would put up with anything just to be able to feast his eyes on her. 'I thought you were going to be killed out there.'

He grinned. 'I told you I used to compete.'

She shook her head, returned his grin. 'Is it fun?'

Oh, yeah. It's fun.

'Why don't you come and find out?'

Her eyes flew to his. 'Out there?'

'No. It's too big out there.' He shook his head. 'There's a little cove on the other side of the island that's protected. There shouldn't be too many people there on a day like today. Are you game?'

She gave a little quick step of glee. 'Really?'

* * *

Spluttering salt water, Cara groaned disgustedly as she fell off the surfboard for the hundredth time. Aidan's powerful arms caught her against him in an effort to prevent her from going under and she tried not to marvel at his strength. Tried not to enjoy his slick flesh sliding against her own.

'This is harder than it looks,' she complained tiredly.

Aidan's eyes locked with hers. Heat sizzled along her cheekbones and arrowed straight to her core.

'Try just feeling the push of the ocean and the sound of the wave behind you and don't worry about getting to your feet.'

'No, I want to stand up!' And this time she vowed to concentrate and not to get distracted by the way Aidan looked in board shorts and nothing else. 'Buff' wasn't quite the word. The man had not an ounce of fat anywhere on his body and his muscles were hard and primed. And yes, she thought on a rush of air, he had hair on his chest. A light smattering that arrowed down to a fine line that bisected the middle of his washboard abs and thickened just before it disappeared beneath the low-slung shorts.

'Okay, but you need to paddle harder.'

What she needed, Cara thought, was to close her eyes and forget all about how she had confided in him yesterday afternoon so that she didn't feel quite so embarrassed by it.

She'd locked herself in her room after he had walked away from her and continued packing. She'd even picked up the phone to ask Dinesh to organise a speedboat to the mainland, wanting to get as far away from her horrible meltdown as possible.

Only, she'd gone for a long walk along the sleepy beach track and realised that if she left she'd be running away again. Running away without a plan. Because once she

left the island the farce of her relationship with Aidan
would be over and they hadn't even discussed how they
were going to 'break up,' and once she was back to her
real life the press would descend on her like wolves going
in for the kill.

Lost in thought a wave caught her unawares and she
went under, the board rolling over the top of her as it got
caught in the white wash. Kicking out from under it she
burst to the surface as Aidan reached her.

God, she was never going to get this!

'Are you okay?'

'Ugh.' She pushed her sodden hair out of her eyes and
made a face. 'Salt water really doesn't taste that good,
does it?'

He laughed. 'You won't make much of a surfer with
that attitude. Have you had enough?'

Somehow she felt that if she were to give up now without having stood up just once on the board it would be a
reflection of her whole life. A reflection of every other
time she had failed to stand up for herself when people had
judged her unfairly. Wondering if she wasn't being a little
bit dramatic she gritted her teeth anyway and gripped the
rails of the board. 'One more.'

'Determination. I like it,' he said, positioning the board
and holding it steady for her.

Cara pulled herself up and lay on her stomach, swear-
ing that this time she would get it.

'Okay, get ready,' Aidan called out beside her. 'The
wave's coming—no, relax and go with it. Let the momen-
tum build. Feel the way it grips you and then find the
sweet spot. Feel how it sucks you backwards and then the
adrenaline rush as it launches you forward. Okay, here it
is—and go!'

With a thrust Cara felt the wave pick up the board as

she surged forward and she relaxed into its grip and submitted to its force. Trembling with excitement she pushed to her knees, steadied and then stumbled to her feet. The board rocked her one way and the wave pulled her another and then, arms outstretched as if she were balancing on a tightrope, Cara found the sweet spot Aidan was talking about and rode the board into shore until its fins dragged on the sandy bottom.

Elated, she jumped off the board and let out a giant whoop, pumping her fist in the air. As the board floated towards the shore she turned and ran back out to Aidan. Without thinking she launched herself into his arms and nearly knocked him over. 'I did it! I did it!'

She wrapped her arms and legs around him and bounced with pure delight. 'Now I know why all those surfers spend hours and hours sitting on the beach waiting for the waves to come up. That was the best feeling in the world.' She couldn't stop herself from babbling. 'I felt like I was floating on air. I felt like I could do anything.'

Cara realised that Aidan wasn't saying anything and then she suddenly became aware that his hands were cupping her bottom and that her legs were wrapped tightly around his lean hips.

Oh, my Lord, and he was…hard, his arousal pressing against her soft belly. An instant rush of liquid fire drenched her lower body and she didn't know whether to straighten her legs or squeeze them tighter.

Her body had a mind of its own and chose the latter and a look of abject pain crossed Aidan's handsome face.

'Oh, I'm sorry, I didn't mean to hurt you.'

Aidan gripped her bottom harder to hold her still and clenched his jaw. 'You didn't…hurt me exactly. Just hold steady before, oh, Jesus, Cara, please stop squeezing your thighs, you're killing me here.'

Cara stilled. She was? With her heart drumming so loudly inside her head Cara couldn't think of anything else except for the man holding her so tightly in his arms.

She was completely aware of their near-nudity and of the warm silky water swirling around their hips. She could feel the fabric of his shorts rough against her core, her bikini so small it was as if it wasn't even there.

Her body felt boneless and she knew that if Aidan were to move his fingers just a little higher he would be able to feel how aroused she was. He would be able to move the tiny strip of fabric to the side and slip his fingers inside her already-parted flesh.

Unable to prevent it, she let out a low moan and her lower body completely ignored Aidan's instructions to hold still and pressed down against the thick ridge of his penis.

He said a word she had once had a nanny wash her mouth out for and then his mouth captured hers and all the pent-up lust she had been trying to keep at bay broke over her like one of the waves surging around them.

Aidan locked one hand in her hair and pressed the other into the small of her back, urging her even closer.

Cara gave herself over to the warm thrust of his tongue and clutched his shoulders, running her hands over his strong back and revelling in the feel of his muscles bunching and releasing as he fought to keep them upright in the surf.

She caught another of his deep groans in her mouth and then she felt his fingers slide beneath the fabric of her bikini bottoms and sanity returned. 'Aidan!'

She pushed at his shoulders when he didn't immediately respond and then his fingers found her wetness and she nearly succumbed to the fever he caused inside of her. 'Aidan, stop,' she gasped weakly.

Those skilful fingers withdrew and she wanted to take back her words and beg him to continue. When he slid them free of her bikini bottoms she made a low keening sound and buried her face against his neck, breathing in his musky male scent and willing her body to stop throbbing.

She felt him lower his face against her hair and breathe deeply. He might have kissed her there, she wasn't sure, but when she made to unwind her legs he stayed her. 'Hold on.' He gritted his teeth. 'Just give me a minute.'

Feeling a thrill race through her when she realised that he was as close to release as she had been, Cara didn't move a muscle. His breathing was ragged beside her ear and after a minute she felt him pull himself back under control. A bird called overhead and she heard the muted sound of distant conversation farther along the beach.

'We're on the beach,' she whispered unnecessarily.

He pulled his head back and looked at her. 'I know.' His eyes, fiercely blue, were filled with hunger. 'I think it's time we got off it.'

Cara heard the question implicit in his statement and she couldn't look away. She knew if she gave him the slightest encouragement he would most likely take her back to their bungalow and make love to her. Her lower body clenched at the thought and her mouth went dry.

Kissing Aidan, touching him, was one of the most electrifying experiences she had ever had in her life. No one else had ever come close to making her feel the same level of excitement that he did. So did she really care that they would be leaving later today and she would likely never see him again? Well, yes, she did. But she also knew that feelings like these didn't come along very often and this might be her only chance to experience something truly magical.

Taking a deep breath she pressed her fingers into his broad shoulders and stared up at him. 'I think so, too.'

CHAPTER THIRTEEN

THE SHORT WALK BACK to their bungalow seemed interminable and Aidan made it as far as kicking the front door closed before turning and pressing Cara up against it. Then he hooked a finger beneath her shoestring bikini strap and paused. His eyes met hers and Cara gave a breathless laugh as he tugged it down.

'For a minute there I thought you were going to fix it,' she said huskily.

'I am.' He curled another finger into its twin and gave another tug. 'It's in my way.'

The tiny triangles of her bikini gave way and Aidan was spellbound.

'You're beautiful,' he said roughly, 'so beautiful.'

She whimpered at his words and threw her arms around his neck, plastering her exquisite breasts up against his naked chest, the firm tips pressing into his hard flesh like a brand. He groaned and crushed her mouth beneath his.

Her taste was like the sweetest nectar and he framed her face and fed from her, thrusting his tongue into her mouth over and over, tasting her again and again. He couldn't get enough of her and drew her up onto her toes and angled her head so that he could explore every inch of her sweetness until she had no secrets left to reveal to him.

'Aidan.' She whispered his name brokenly, her smoky

voice filled with a desperate yearning. A desperate yearning he returned.

She stared up at him, trying to catch her breath, her aqua blue eyes searching.

He stilled.

'Take out your contact lenses,' he said roughly. He didn't give a damn who she was channelling today but he wanted to know that it was her he was making love to. She could colour her hair whatever colour she wanted, wear whatever style of clothing she wanted, but on this he would not compromise. In this moment she would not hide herself from him.

She paused, uncertainty crossing her lovely face. He circled his hands around her throat and tilted her chin up with his thumbs. 'I want to see you, Cara. I want to watch your eyes darken when I fit myself inside you for the first time. I want to watch them glaze over when you come for me.'

Breathing shallowly, she reached up between them and ducked her head as she slid first one small disc and then the other out of her eyes.

Then she looked up at him and his heart kicked against his ribs. His mind went blank, just as it had done in that moment at the airport when he'd gripped her upper arms after she'd stepped into his path. Then, he'd presumed that he had just been aggravated with her. Now...now...he just stared into eyes of the deepest, darkest brown. Rich and glossy like the colour of freshly roasted coffee beans. Warm, sincere and devastatingly beautiful.

She blinked her gaze to the side as if embarrassed and suddenly he was back in the real world with a seminaked, sun-warmed woman in his arms. 'Please promise me you won't ever wear contact lenses around me again,' he said thickly.

She coloured and moistened her lips so he did what

any man would do. He bent his head and took her mouth again. Her lips trembled beneath the force of his but he'd be damned if he'd give her the opportunity to close off from him again so he deepened the kiss even more. Filled her mouth with his essence and slid his hands to her waist. She whimpered and melted into him.

At the feel of those small breasts nestling against his chest he broke from her mouth and kissed his way down her neck, arching her back over his arm so that her breasts were tilted upwards, his for the taking. He watched her as he rolled his tongue over first one rigid peak and then the other. Her brown eyes darkened and her dense lashes drooped over them. 'Watch me,' he commanded, waiting for her to peel her eyes open once again, and then he fastened his mouth over one tight tip and sucked her deep into his mouth.

She cried out and curled her hands into his hair. He pushed her against the door and fell to his knees in front of her. Her sexy tattoo beckoned and he ran his tongue around it and had to press his hands into her hips when she bucked against him. He looked up to find her slumberous gaze watching his tongue dip in and out of her navel.

The primal need to take her bit deep and he had to take a moment to steady himself. He was iron-bar hard and his body had one aim. To mate with her. To yank her to the floorboards and sink into her without preamble. Without finesse. Hell, without any foreplay.

Forcing himself back from an edge he'd never found himself close to before he slid her bikini bottoms down her legs and tossed them away. Then he nuzzled her silky curls, breathed her warm woman's scent into his blood and opened her for his mouth.

She whimpered his name and lust shot through him; he'd never enjoyed playing with and torturing a woman so much. Almost immediately he could feel her body start to quake as it reached the brink of pleasure and he pulled back, wanting this first time when she came to be inside her. Joined with her.

Not quite steady on his feet he rose and lashed his mouth over hers. She met his kiss with an urgency that matched his own, her hands clutching at his neck and shoulders.

'Aidan, please…'

'Undo my shorts,' he commanded thickly.

She did, her unsteady fingers fumbling first with the laces and then finally, thank God, finally, she peeled open the Velcro.

'Oh, my.' Her voice was hoarse as she pulled him free of his clothing and clutched him in her tight fist. 'You feel amazing.'

Aidan moved his hands to cup her and gently pushed a finger into her soft heat, thrusting in and out, preparing her for his possession. Even around his finger she felt snug. Wet. *Perfect*.

Growling, he slid urgent hands to her thighs and lifted her, parting her. Her coconut-scented breasts rubbed against his chin and he made a deep, animalistic sound as he positioned himself and penetrated her tight sheath for the first time.

It was like being thrown into the centre of a giant flame. His body burned with a fever that rattled the chains of his self-control. Sweat broke out over his skin and his legs felt perilously weak. Life as he knew it ceased to exist. There was only this moment. This woman.

Her startled gasp brought him back into himself and he held still, sweat beading on his brow as he gave her time to get used to the feel of him filling her. God knew the feel of her was turning him inside out. The need to pound into her a driving force he had to concentrate to master.

Unable to wait another minute he began to move slowly

and closed his eyes against the sweet bliss of her tight body gripping him and pulling him deeper, as deep as he could go.

Then he remembered contraception and swore.

The force of the four-letter word made her rise up on him in surprise and it was all he could do not to shove her back down and finish the job.

Her hands squeezed around his shoulders. 'Please, Aidan, don't—'

'Condom,' he muttered between rough breaths.

'Oh.'

'Oh' was right. When was the last time he'd forgotten one of those?

'Are you protected?'

She shook her head and her body gripped his. He groaned, clenched his teeth and pulled slowly out of her.

Picking her up, he dropped her onto the single bed in his room.

She didn't move, her long limbs sprawled helplessly as she watched him roll a condom on.

Then he climbed onto the bed and on top of her. He took a moment to cup her jaw. Kiss her. Then he widened her legs and powered back into her, his eyes locked with hers as he took in every nuance of her response to him. Shock. Wonder. *Delight*.

And she was so responsive. Wrapping her long legs around his hips and holding him to her. Ignoring the fact that he'd never felt this good, never wanted a woman as much, he surged into her again and again until her harsh cries of completion filled his ears and only then did he let himself go completely.

When they woke it was dark outside. Cara stretched and felt two hair-roughened legs tangled with her own and stilled. He had one arm around her, anchoring her to his side, her head pillowed on his chest. It felt good. So good. *Too good.*

She lay still, breathing in the scent of sweat and man. She wanted to stay but she knew that nothing this good ever lasted.

Memories came rushing back and her mind reeled. Had she ever felt like that before? Had she ever felt so completely taken by a man? So completely desired? Had lying in a man's arms ever felt so *wonderful*?

No.

No to all of the above. Which was beyond concerning.

Trying not to wake him she inched out of bed and headed for her room on slightly shaky legs.

Even though it was dark she didn't bother turning on a light until she reached the bathroom.

When she did she glanced at herself in the mirror and released a slow breath. Her hair was a mess and her eyes were dark. Brown. They looked like two fathomless pools of churning emotion.

Had she just made a huge mistake?

'You're thinking this has been a huge mistake.'

Startled, Cara whirled around at the sound of Aidan's deep voice and snatched a towel off the rail to hold in front of her body. Silly, really, when he had already seen all of her. Touched all of her... Kissed all of her...

He leaned against the doorjamb wearing nothing but the board shorts from earlier, the Velcro hastily pulled together and doing little to hide the bulge beneath. Cara swallowed hard. He was so rampantly male he took her breath away just looking at him.

'Aren't you?' she asked, her voice husky from lack of use.

'Don't worry about what *I'm* thinking.' His voice brought her eyes back to his. 'What are *you* thinking?'

That this is all a huge mistake.

And that she couldn't stop wondering what he was thinking. It seemed more important than her own view on it. How silly was that?

'You're too sensitive, Cara.' Her sister's words came back to her.

Was she? Was she being that now?

And why couldn't she be honest? Why couldn't she say that she was worried that she had felt too much in his arms earlier? That she was sure that no man would ever make her feel the way Aidan did again, which scared the pants off her.

Somehow she wasn't that brave. She'd rather live in the grey world of half-truths than confront things and be hurt by them.

Unfortunately this man was more the confront-things-head-on type.

'If it's important for you to know what I'm thinking,' he said, 'then I'm thinking that tonight—or is it last night?—was sensational.'

'Oh.' Her hands tightened around the towel.

'And that this doesn't need to be complex. We can keep everything nice and simple.'

'Simple?' She knew there was a warning implicit in those words. A warning for her not to lose her heart most likely but her body really didn't care.

'Yeah.' He moved closer. 'Simple.' A slow smile curled the edges of his lips. He stopped an inch away from touching her and smoothed her hair back behind her ears, catching one of her tiny braids between his fingers. 'We're two adults who share an explosive sexual chemistry that I, for one, am not finished exploring.'

He leaned forward and kissed the corner of her lips. He touched her there briefly with his tongue before transferring his attention to the other side. Liquid heat pooled low in her pelvis and Cara closed her eyes to savour the sensations.

'I'm not ready to go back to Sydney yet, either,' he surprised her by adding. 'I haven't had a holiday for a long time. I thought I might try and embrace a little Fiji time. Why don't you embrace it with me?'

Why didn't she? Because things had a tendency to go wrong for her.

He lifted his mouth from hers and shifted slightly back from her. 'No pressure.'

No pressure. Is that what she needed? She didn't know. She only knew that she needed him.

'I have to be in London by Sunday for the Demarche unveiling,' she reminded him.

He nuzzled her neck and her pulse jumped in her throat. 'Then we'll leave Friday. Is that soon enough for you?'

'Yes, but…"we"?'

'You said you don't like being alone. Unless of course you have another date lined up?'

'No.' *God.* 'I'd like you to come with me.'

'Good, that's settled.' His voice was a hot whisper along her skin, making her nerve endings strain for more. 'Now we just have one more thing to settle.'

Cara slid her hands into his thick hair and loved the feel of its soft springiness. Was he seriously going to come with her to London? She couldn't stop the smile from splitting across her face and she pushed aside the little voice in her head that reminded her that he didn't believe in true love. 'Oh? What's that?'

His hands slid to her waist and he stepped her backwards, towards the shower. 'The island frowns on water wastage. I didn't want to say anything before but…' He turned on the shower and pulled her towel away. 'I think we should consider sharing.'

'Really?'

His gaze drifted over her body. 'It's a very serious offense.'

'Well, I certainly don't want to offend anyone….' Cara demurred.

'Glad to hear it. So…' He smiled. Stepped forward and crowded her back.

Knowing she was probably going to get hurt, knowing that there was only one way this could end, Cara felt helpless in the face of his raw masculinity and her own deep yearning and backed into the shower stall.

Breathless, she watched Aidan shuck out of his shorts and pick up the soap. He rubbed it between his big hands until they were thick with bubbles.

'Here.' He offered it to her. 'Hold this.'

She took it and he cupped soapy hands around her shoulders, slowly making small circles south. Her nipples stiffened and Cara squeezed the soap as he eventually reached them and tugged. She moaned and bit her lower lip as he continued soaping her torso and between her thighs.

Then he took down the nozzle from the shower and sprayed her aching body. Cara collapsed back against the wet tiles as he cupped her and rinsed the soap away. Then he fell to his knees and took her with his mouth and she nearly lost it, gripping his head with her hands to try and keep herself upright.

The sound of the soap hitting the tiles brought a husky laugh from him and she dragged him upwards and slid her soapy hand around his impressive erection.

Aidan growled and pressed the nozzle more firmly against her core. When Cara started undulating against it he let it swing against the wall and lifted her and thrust himself inside her with one smooth motion.

Cara felt her womb contract as she gripped him. This was pleasure at its most elemental and fulfilling and she arched her back and started to ride him.

'Christ, Cara.' Aidan released her breast and braced a hand behind her on the tiles as if he couldn't hold them up. 'You feel…' He pulled back and surged forward. 'Fantastic.'

Cara gasped, her body convulsing, her mind spinning into another vortex as Aidan joined her in the most exquisite release.

CHAPTER FOURTEEN

CARA STARED AT her reflection in the bathroom mirror and wondered if she'd done the right thing in colouring her hair. Or having the five-star spa colour it for her.

It had been a spur-of-the-moment decision after Aidan had booked her in for an afternoon of relaxation. 'We're going somewhere special tonight,' he'd said. 'Dress up.'

She'd been excited all day wondering how he was going to top the past three blissful days where daylight had slipped into night and then night had miraculously slipped back into day.

When the sun came up they ate a quick breakfast— usually in bed—and walked around the island, sometimes stopping to kayak in the bay or snorkel around the shallows. By afternoon they had usually collapsed into a hammock, or their king-size bed where Aidan had threatened more than once that he was going to tie her up the next time he wasn't so exhausted from their lovemaking.

On this particular day Aidan had hired a yacht. They'd sailed it to a nearby island that was deserted and had a picnic on the beach. Made love. Then Aidan had produced scuba-diving gear and taken her down into the clear depths of the ocean where twelve feet looked like three.

It was another world. A secret world. At once quiet and enclosed and yet alive with activity. Brightly coloured fish ducked in and around coral that looked like it belonged in fairyland.

Aidan had picked up various animals from the seabed. A starfish that was stiff as rubber but somehow still malleable and an oblong brown shape—he'd later informed her was a sea cucumber—that looked like a brick and was as soft as a sponge to the touch. Then he'd put her hand out to a school of curious clownfish and she'd squealed and jerked back into his arms when they had come close enough to nip her.

She grinned at the memory.

She'd lost her mouthpiece that time and her mask had filled with water. She should have panicked but Aidan's arms had come around her and he had showed her how to clear her mask underwater and then leaned in and kissed her, breathing oxygen into her mouth before refitting her mouthpiece.

Then he grabbed her hand and they'd swam lazily back to the boat where they'd stretched out on the sun-warmed deck and finished off the chocolate and champagne.

It had been straight out of a fantasy and only the looming sense that, actually, this wasn't real life for either of them and that in two days' time they would have to leave kept her grounded in reality.

Or so she tried to tell herself. It was hard not to get swept away by the romance of the island. And probably the only thing that had marred the day was when the conversation had drifted around to family.

She'd just finished telling him about the time her twin brothers had chased her and threatened to throw her in the lake—after she'd caught them drinking alcohol when they were thirteen—when she asked Aidan about his family life.

'No, no siblings,' he'd said.

They'd been lying on the deck utterly exhausted after the scuba diving. Or at least she had been. 'So what was it like where you grew up?' she asked, rolling onto her side to look down at him.

'Nothing special,' he said, keeping his eyes closed.

Cara had felt his slight withdrawal and tried to tell herself that she had imagined it and asked why he didn't like talking about his childhood.

'I don't mind.' He'd said it casually, crossing one muscular arm over his face as if to shield his closed eyes from the overhead sun.

'So did you grow up in a big house? A little house? Did you go to an expensive boys' school or an expensive co-ed?'

'No expensive school. I was a kid from the western suburbs before they became cashed up. Originally my dad was a tradie who started a free newspaper before they were popular and made a business out of it.'

'Entrepreneurial,' she'd said, brushing a few grains of sand that had stubbornly clung to the dark hair on his forearm. 'Is that where you get your business brain from?'

'Something like that.' He'd lifted her hand and studied it. 'My mother certainly appreciated the shift from blue-collar to white-collar and before you know it goodbye western suburbs and hello Rose Bay.'

'You don't sound like you liked the move very much.'

His fingers almost absently laced with hers and he stared at the overhead sky as if he'd never noticed it before and didn't like what he was looking at. 'A lot changed after that. My mother left.'

'Oh, I'm sorry. Was it a bad break-up?'

He stared at their entwined fingers as if he didn't understand how they had got like that. 'It's fine, Cara. I was old enough to handle it.'

Cara, too, studied her small, pale hand engulfed in his much larger one. 'Do you still see her?'

'No. She died in a car accident eighteen months ago. But I'll tell you something.' He stopped and rolled over so quickly Cara was on her back and blinking up at him before she'd even taken her next breath. 'Boring conversation always makes me horny.'

She'd wanted to ask more, of course, but he'd already reached behind her and tilted her lower body into his and rational thought had been usurped by instant arousal.

It hadn't been so much a sharing of information, she realised now, but more a man suffering through an inquisition.

It made her realise that he didn't trust her as much as she trusted him and she'd wanted him to. She'd heard the bitterness in his voice when he mentioned his mother and she wondered if his mother leaving was one of the reasons he didn't believe in long-term relationships. It would make sense. Especially if the break-up had been acrimonious, which she was almost certain it must have been.

And to know that his mother had died and he'd never see her again was so sad....

Deciding not to dwell on anything that could bring her mood down, Cara took one more glance at her reflection and headed out into the living room.

Aidan was already dressed. Denim jeans that hugged his strong thighs, a white open-necked shirt. His hair was slightly damp and his feet bare. He sat slouched in the deep sofa watching some sort of sports game on the TV and Cara's mouth instantly dried. He was devastating and she thought it would take a hundred years of looking at him to maybe, just maybe, get used to the impact of his masculine presence.

His true blue eyes held hers for a second and then swept

down over her figure. She felt more nervous than she could
ever remember feeling and she did a little twirl to hide it.
'How do I look?'

'Stunning.'

'My hair is brown,' she said, more than a little self-
conscious. 'This is pretty close to my natural colour. In
fact, if it were to grow out I doubt you'd see any difference.'

'Stop worrying. You look incredible.'

'You don't think I look like a Stepford wife?'

Aidan laughed and unfolded from the sofa and came
towards her. 'No, I don't.'

Cara could see his chest rising and falling with his
heavy breaths and when he stopped in front of her his
eyes locked on to her mouth. 'Does that stuff smudge?'

'It's called lipstick.' She laughed. 'And yes, it will.'

'Damn, then I'll have to satisfy myself with your neck
instead.'

Cara clutched his wide shoulders as he pulled her in
close and bent to the raging pulse point in her neck. She
moaned and her body turned boneless as she felt the hard
ridge of him press against her. Would it always be like
this? she thought, breathless. Would it always be so all-
encompassing?

It was Aidan who finally raised his head, his gaze lin-
gering on her mouth. 'How much do you care about that
lipstick?'

'I don't, but aren't we supposed to be somewhere?' she
reminded him.

'Oh, yeah.' He groaned and reluctantly released her
before walking to a small table with a mirror above it.
'Come here.'

Cara saw the black velvet jewellery case on the top.
Happy tears spiked behind her eyes and she walked towards him as if in a daze. 'You bought me something?'

'A memento,' he said gruffly. 'Turn around.'

Feeling choked, Cara did, her heart trying to beat its way out of her chest. Was it a memento of her time on the island or her time with him?

As if in answer to her silent questions, he said, 'I figure you deserve something nice after last weekend.'

Oh, so it was a pity present? Her eyes sought his out in the mirror but he was looking at the box and not her. Fixing a smile on her face she took it as a good reminder that this was not a romance novel and that imagining that Aidan had meant anything more by the gesture would be truly foolish on her part.

'Jenny's pearls,' she said softly, focusing on the necklace and what it didn't mean. She stroked the single layer of glowing silver-grey pearls similar to the ones she had admired so much the other day. 'It's beautiful. I didn't see this one.'

'It's one of her earlier pieces.' He reached around and took her hand and circled her wrist with a matching bracelet.

'Oh, Aidan. You shouldn't have.'

'Esther wouldn't let me leave without it. And...' He reached into the box once more. 'Earrings.'

Cara pressed her hand to her chest as he revealed twin gunmetal grey pearls. 'I don't know what to say.'

She felt her lower lip quiver and stuck her teeth into it.

'Don't cry, or I'll take it all back,' he said gruffly, pulling her lip free from her teeth.

Cara swallowed the emotion bubbling away inside of her and decided to suppress the instinct to throw her arms around his neck and instead picked up the earrings and started fastening them in her ears. 'I love them. Thank you. I've been thinking a lot lately about the future,' she said, wanting to fill the void that had once again opened up inside her. 'And I think one day I'll open a little shop. Do you think Jenny would be interested in collaborating with me?'

'She might. But what about modelling?'

'Mmm, I like it but…I think I'm better at putting combinations of outfits together than actually wearing them.'

'I agree,' he said seriously. 'You look terrible in clothes. From now on I think you should go around naked.'

Cara rolled her eyes. 'I'm serious. I love the idea of selling offbeat, hard-to-find pieces that women treasure and keep for ever.'

'That's because you're a hoarder.'

'How do you know that?'

'You travel with ten suitcases.'

She smiled. 'I *am* a hoarder. When I was younger I could never clean out my cupboard and I refused to throw anything out. One summer I came home and my nanny at the time had gone through my things and tossed out anything she thought was junk. I was devastated.'

He kissed her softly on the mouth and when she leaned into him he took a deep breath and stepped back. 'If we don't leave right now we won't be going. What's it to be?'

'Well, that depends on what you have organised.'

Aidan pulled a piece of paper out of his pocket.

It was a theatre flyer from an English group touring the Australasian region.

'Romeo and Juliet?' She looked up at him and knew her eyes were sparkling with pleasure. 'Seriously? What made you choose this?'

Aidan gave a pained groan. 'I take it from the glow in your eyes that you've chosen to go out.'

Cara smiled at his tortured expression. 'Well, I do love the theatre and it's only for a couple of hours….'

'Right then.' He grabbed her hand and headed for the door. 'Let's get this over with.'

Cara laughed as he pulled her towards the door. 'You sound like you're about to make a trip to the dentist.'

'Might be better,' he grumbled good-naturedly.

'Are you saying that you don't like Shakespeare?'

He guided her towards the dune buggy parked outside the entrance to their bungalow. 'Hey, I'm just a boy from the western suburbs deep down.'

No, he wasn't. He was sophisticated and charming and honourable. He was a man you could rely on to always be there if he gave his word that he would.

'Just don't cry,' he warned her as he put the buggy into gear. 'The first sign of tears and we're gone.'

Cara reached across the space and laid her hand on his arm. 'Thank you,' she said softly. 'For everything.'

'You promised me you wouldn't cry,' Aidan complained as they climbed back into the buggy.

Cara sniffed. 'Technically I didn't actually promise and I'm really trying not to but it was so beautiful. Didn't you think?'

Aidan smoothed a tear from her cheek. 'I'm going to have to start packing tissues around you.'

'No matter how many times I see it,' Cara said, 'I wish Juliet had been the type to jump up and run after both their families and wring their necks for being so small-minded that they couldn't put the past behind them instead of killing herself. Then she could have come back and they would have been together for ever.'

'For ever?' A strange light entered his eyes that looked a little like fear.

'Of course. They loved each other.'

'You buy Hallmark cards, as well, right?' he teased, re-minding Cara of what he thought of forever after.

'Actually, I draw my own.'

He straightened her necklace, a crooked smile on his face. 'Juliet wasn't the type to seek vengeance because she was sweet and generous. Giving.'

'She needed to grow a backbone.'

'That was Romeo's job. He should have stood up for her.'

Cara smiled sadly. 'And that's why it's called fiction.'

Aidan scooped her up into his arms and shouldered open the door to the bungalow. It had become like their home away from home, an intimate cocoon where they wrapped themselves around each other every night.

He stripped her bare and Cara groaned as he started to make slow, passionate love to her.

Before he turned her into a quivering mess unable to do anything but lie back and take whatever he wanted to give her, she rolled them over and straddled his waist.

He gazed up at her, his hands behind his head, his blue eyes dark and lazy.

She leaned forward and placed her hands on his chest, curling her nails into the soft hair there, her eyes drifting over his handsome face. She reached forward and traced her finger over his eyebrows and down the straight ridge of his nose.

Warmth stole through her and her heart seemed to swell behind her chest. She let her fingers drift across his sensual lips and lightly scratched the stubble that had formed on his tanned jaw. He breathed deeply, his nostrils flaring, and Cara realised with a start that she had fallen in love with him.

Thrillingly, wonderfully, joyously, impossibly in love with him.

The realisation floored her. She searched her brain for other times she had imagined herself in love but she couldn't think of a single time that she had felt like this. As if her heart was about to burst.

Was it even possible to fall in love with someone so quickly? 'You know, I know we've both embraced Fiji time,' Aidan drawled, bringing his hands out from behind his head to mould around her hips. 'But I think now you're taking things a little far.'

Cara sucked in a steadying breath.

Was he falling for her, too? Could it be possible?

She made a face. Not likely and she wasn't nearly brave enough to ask. Wasn't brave enough to even explore her own feelings in this moment. So she didn't. Instead she slid down his body and let herself be swept away by his touch and his taste.

Tomorrow. Tomorrow would be soon enough to deal with her feelings.

Unfortunately tomorrow came all too quickly with the bright sunshine streaming in through the window and Aidan's angry voice carrying from the living room.

Blinking open sleepy eyes, Cara pulled on the shirt Aidan had discarded the night before and padded down the hallway to investigate.

Aidan was wearing his old board shorts and nothing else, the phone attached to one ear and his morning coffee gripped in the other.

'He won't get it. I'll make sure of it.' He paused. 'Yes, personally. Have Sam ready the plane. And set up a meeting with the AFL board first thing tomorrow morning.'

When he rang off he tossed his phone onto the dining table and that was when he noticed Cara standing in the doorway.

She tried not to think the worst, but her heart was hammering inside her chest.

'Problems?'

'You could say that.' He took a gulp of coffee and grimaced. 'I have to return to Australia.'

'Yes, I heard.'

When he didn't say anything more, just stared out the window, Cara felt a chill come over her body. 'What's the AFL?'

He didn't turn around. 'The Australian Football League.'

'And they're in trouble?'

'No, we're in trouble.' His words were clipped. Impenetrable. 'KMG has had the AFL broadcasting rights for sixteen years. It's the most lucrative TV deal in the country and now Martin Ellery has put in a hostile bid for it.'

'Martin Ellery?'

'I don't want to discuss it, Cara.'

He stalked past her and the chill she'd felt moments before turned to ice. All of a sudden she felt like they were back at the casino and he was once again the man who had dragged her to his room and looked at her with such contempt.

Power and focused determination vibrated in the long lines of his lean body and she felt a little bit like a prisoner walking towards their own execution as she followed him into the main bedroom. 'Is that why you dislike him so much?'

Aidan threw his clothes out of the cupboard and onto the bed. 'I told you I don't want to talk about it.'

Cara stood poised in the doorway, unsure about what to do. Unsure about how to reach him, or if she should even try. His attitude had relegated her to the slush pile along with all the other hopefuls in his life.

'I have the Demarche launch in two days,' she said, hating the tentative note in her voice but unable to change it. 'I thought…I thought you were going to come with me.'

He looked up, but Cara sensed that he wasn't really seeing her. 'I can't now. This is important.'

'You can't delegate?' she asked lightly. 'I mean, can't Ben go to the meeting? He seems really capable.'

'No,' he said, too softly. 'Ben cannot stand in for me. Nobody else can do it. I have to.'

'Why?' she asked. 'Why does it always have to be you?'

'Because if you're not in control things go wrong.' The look in his eyes was hard and flat. Unreachable. 'This week, I've let things slip and…that's never a good thing.'

'Did that happen to you in the past?'

He looked like he was grinding nails, his frustration at her continued questioning palpable. Cara had to fight her instinct to bury her head and walk away. This seemed too important for her to do that.

'It happened to my father.' He paused. 'You want to know why I hate Ellery?' He ran an agitated hand through his hair. 'Twelve months ago almost to the day my father took his own life and it was Ellery's fault.'

'Oh, Aidan, I'm so sorry.'

Aidan continued as if he hadn't heard her. 'He never regained consciousness after swallowing a bottle of pills, although the hospital was hopeful at the time. I sat with him for three days, watching him die.'

He wasn't looking at her now and Cara held herself completely still, waiting for him to continue. When he didn't she moved closer to him. 'Why did he… Why…' Cara didn't know what to say in the face of such a tragedy. 'Did he leave a note?'

'He didn't have to,' Aidan said bitterly. 'He killed himself because my mother wasn't coming back.'

'You mean because she died.'

He nodded curtly. 'Even though she had left him years before, he let his feelings for her dominate his whole life.'

Cara's brow pleated. 'Oh, I'm sorry. I don't know what to say.'

'There's nothing to say. Fourteen years ago she saw a better deal and she took it and my father fell apart. Then he killed himself. End of story.'

But it wasn't the end of the story and something in Aidan's voice alerted her to the sense that there was more going on here.

'You said he died because of Martin Ellery. He was the man your mother left him for, wasn't he?'

'Give the girl a gold star,' he said bitterly. 'Yes, my mother left with him. He was my father's business partner and friend before he embezzled money and nearly destroyed my father's company.'

'Oh, that's horrible.' Cara went to his side and laid her head against the rigid wall of muscles on his back. 'I can see now why you haven't been able to move on from this. Why you don't want to let him win.'

'Can you?'

'Yes, and I'll come with you.'

Aidan tensed and turned towards her. 'You'll what?'

'I'll come with you. I didn't like Martin Ellery on sight and I want to support you.'

He rubbed a hand reflexively over his pectoral muscles. 'What about the Demarche party?'

'I think it's more important to be with you at a time when you're so emotional.'

He stepped farther away from her and Cara's palms felt instantly cold without his heat against them.

'I'm not emotional, Cara. I'm never emotional about business.'

'Aidan, I—'

'I thought your career was important to you.' He paced across the room, his normally loose-legged gait stiff in his agitation. 'I thought the whole purpose of you being here was to save your reputation and impress your father.'

'It was….' Cara swallowed, her head swimming at the implication behind his less than enthusiastic response to her suggestion. 'I just… I thought…' What had she thought? That this had become real? That he returned her feelings? God, she felt like an idiot.

He was rejecting her. The man who always kept his promise had broken the one he had made to her….

Cara turned away and caught sight of her reflection in the glass windows. She was naked except for his shirt, but it wasn't her attire that caught her attention. It was her hair. Brown. Like her eyes. It hadn't been like that for five years. She'd been every shade of blonde. She'd been red, burgundy, black, pink….

She stared at her pensive expression, her neat hair.

She looked like a Stepford wife in training.

Wife?

A harsh sound of humiliation nearly broke from her throat. Aidan wasn't offering her marriage. He wasn't even offering her a real relationship. He had done her a favour in bringing her to Fiji. Then he'd decided to take some time out from his busy schedule and because he'd asked her to stay she had started spinning castles in the air.

Oh, God. She shook her head. It was time to reassert herself. Time to start living her life again. If she didn't, if she went with him now and waited for him to end it with her… She shuddered as pain lanced her heart. Already it was unimaginable to be without him but she knew that feeling would fade.

How often as a young girl had she dressed in a pretty

dress anticipating the arrival of her father at Chatsfield House and been quietly devastated when he had barely acknowledged her and kept on going. He'd never drawn her into a hug, or swung her in the air, or tugged her onto his knee.

She'd gotten over that, hadn't she?

She heard Aidan curse behind her and she tried to clear the mental fog her mind wanted to curl up and die in.

'You're right,' she said woodenly. 'I don't know what I was thinking.'

'Dammit, Cara, don't look at me like that. We can talk about this another time.'

Instinctively striving for calm, Cara knew it was time to grow a thick skin. 'Talk about what?'

'Look, I need a clear head right now and getting mired down in…*this* isn't doing it for me.'

He said *'this'* as if it was a different kind of four-letter word and it gave Cara the strength to finally face reality.

'Well, *this*.' She mimicked his tone lightly. 'Meant quite a bit to me. More, clearly, than it meant to you.'

'Oh, hell.' He plunged two hands through his hair at once. 'We agreed to keep things simple, Cara. Remember?'

'By simple I take it you mean that I shouldn't care about what happens to you?' Her smile was hollow. 'Sorry. I didn't get that part of the memo.'

'Cara, you're a wonderful girl. You're smart and funny and loyal and…' His frown deepened. 'You deserve to find someone special. Someone who loves you.'

Cara felt like someone had just punched her in the stomach. Could he make it any plainer that he wasn't that man?

'I agree.' She strove for calm so that he wouldn't guess that she felt completely numb inside. Physically and emotionally numb, her brain swirling like a plastic bag in a tornado. 'So thank you for rescuing me and for the wonderful week. I wish you… I'll just…' She took a deep breath. 'Grab my stuff.'

She didn't hear him come up behind her in her room but she felt his frustration in the bite of his fingers on her shoulders. She welcomed the small pain because it gave her something to focus on other than the pain in her chest.

'Cara, I just can't handle emotional complications. I need a clear head.'

God, so did she. She needed a clear head to get over him.

'I understand.' *It's not me, it's you.* If it hadn't hurt so much it might be funny. 'And it's fine. Really. I just forgot that I had promised myself I wouldn't get involved with a man who proved my sister's rule but I did. My fault, not yours.'

'Rule? What—? Oh.' His brow furrowed and then she saw the moment he remembered their earlier conversation about love and commitment. 'That rule, right.'

He glanced away from her and that was the nail that sealed it for her. They both knew without having to verbalise it that this had only been short term. Cara had pulled the blinkers over her eyes for a time but in the end it had gone exactly as she had known it would. 'Goodbye, Aidan, and…good luck with Martin Ellery.'

He didn't look at her, just continued to stare out the window, and as the silence grew, Cara willed him to turn around and tell her that he'd just realised that he couldn't let her go. That life wouldn't be the same without her. That he wanted her beyond measure.

'Take the jet.'

And there it was. Irrefutable proof that fairytales, in fact, did not come true.

'No, your situation is more important than mine. I'll catch a commercial flight.'

Trying not to let him see that her world felt like it had just broken open like a fissure in an earthquake, she started moving her luggage to the door.

'Leave those. I'll organise it.' He sounded frustrated and irritable but when Cara glanced up at him his face was completely devoid of emotion. It gave her the confidence that her decision was the right one because eventually she knew that being with someone who locked himself so firmly away like that would eat away at her self-esteem. 'And, Cara, take the damned jet.'

When she was on the plane she caught sight of her reflection again and that was when she realised that she had stripped herself bare for him. She had stripped away every one of her protective layers and he still didn't want her. She didn't think she could cry all the way home, but apparently she could.

CHAPTER FIFTEEN

THE DAMNED WOMAN hadn't taken the jet. It still irked him that she had disobeyed him like that. When his pilot had called with the information, Aidan had tried to contact her but he didn't have her mobile phone number.

He'd nearly laughed. He'd been intimate with her—hell, he'd told her things he'd never spoken about to another living soul—and he didn't even have her damned phone number. It seemed somehow absurd.

And what was even more absurd was that he was in the middle of heated negotiations to save his rights to the AFL broadcast and all he could think about was Cara.

His gut tightened. He could still see the hurt expression on her face when he'd told her to take the jet. But, hell, what else was he supposed to have said? He knew she'd wanted him to go to London with her but…he couldn't. He'd had to fight Ellery on this. Especially since the week before he'd let him win. He couldn't do that again.

He pushed up from his chair and the conversation floating around him ceased. He looked down at twelve pairs of eyes staring back at him. 'Keep going,' he said, crossing to the window and staring out at the Sydney Opera House shining in the sun.

And she was dead wrong in what she had said. He

wasn't emotional over Ellery. Yes, he blamed the man for what he'd done to his parents but…

Hell.

This *was* emotional.

How could he deny it when his gut churned every time he thought about it? It was the same sickening feeling he'd experienced when he'd watched Cara try to hold herself together the day before.

And where was she now? Back in England? No, she wouldn't have landed yet. Was she upset? Worried about the launch party tomorrow night?

The trouble was he'd gotten in too deep with Cara. He'd known that the minute he'd wanted to haul her into his arms to take the hurt out of her eyes. But how could he do that when making things right for her was completely wrong for him?

Relationships just weren't his thing. After his parents' divorce he'd vowed to never let emotion drive his decision-making. Seeing his father fall apart after he'd nearly lost everything had gutted him.

It had hardened him. And yesterday he'd realised that he had needed to cut ties with Cara or he'd be no better off than his father, a man he'd loved but who he had ultimately not respected…. Pain swelled behind his breastbone.

And why couldn't he stop thinking about this? He was in the middle of a meeting, for God's sake.

'I can see why you haven't been able to move on from this. Why you don't want to let him win.'

Hell, yes, he wanted justice.

The hollow feeling he'd experienced at the casino table right before he'd thrown Ellery's money back at him returned.

Because no matter what he did to Ellery it wouldn't change the past. Nothing could do that. And Aidan realised that pursuing him with such focused determination made him no better than the man he was chasing.

Forgiveness.

The word whispered over him as if Cara was actually in the room with him.

And that was when he realised why she had scared him so much. Why he felt like he had been running from the minute he'd met her. He'd fallen in love with her. And dammit if she wasn't right. When you fell in love, truly in love, you couldn't not be with that person.

'Aidan?'

Aidan looked across the table at Ben and realised he had no idea what was going on in the meeting.

He leaned back against the window and gripped the ledge. 'Gentlemen, if you would all excuse me, I would like to speak with Ben James alone for a moment.'

The board members blinked almost in unison, then one by one they slowly rose and exited the room.

Ben let out a low whistle. 'I'm not sure anyone's ever asked the AFL board to wait in the hallway like that before. Hell of a way to convince them to reject Ellery's bid. What the blazes is going on?'

Aidan pushed away from the window and reached for his jacket. 'I need you to run the meeting.'

'You need me to…' Ben stopped. 'Why?'

'I have somewhere I need to be.'

'Right now?'

Aidan gave him a faint smile. 'I made a bad decision yesterday and now that I know it I have to fix it straightaway.'

Ben shook his head. 'Do I know about this decision? Do you need my input?'

Aidan smiled. 'Only to hold the fort while I'm gone.'

'What if we lose the bid?' Ben said quickly. 'I can tell

you, Aidan, I feel pretty confident to stand in for you on most things but I know how important this is. If I lose it…'

Aidan buttoned his jacket. 'It won't matter.'

Ben stared at him. 'Mate, are you sure you're okay?'

Aidan smiled. 'Yes, I think, finally, maybe I am.'

'Are you sure you're okay?'

Cara looked up at Lucilla, who had insisted on accompanying her to the Demarche launch party. Despite the slight tiredness around her sister's eyes, Lucilla looked stunning. She'd look even more so with her hair down but no amount of nagging could convince Lucilla to do anything other than tie it back out of her way. Sighing, Cara wondered how to answer her sister's concerned question.

Yes, she was okay, even though she felt slightly sick in the stomach. The model she was competing against to win the contract was one of the most beautiful women Cara had ever seen. And one of the nicest. On a scale of one to ten Cara put Serena Bhattessa at eleven and herself at maybe a seven. On a good day.

In fact, Cara wasn't even sure why she was in the running anymore and it bothered her that she wasn't more bothered by the thought of losing the contract. This was what she wanted, wasn't it? This was why she had left Aidan.

Well, no, this wasn't why she had left Aidan. In fact, she hadn't wanted to leave him. She'd wanted to go to Sydney with him. And she probably would be there right now if Aidan had wanted her with him.

She felt her throat constrict. She promised herself that she wouldn't think of him for the next three hours at least.

So far she'd lasted five minutes.

'Never better,' she finally answered Lucilla, smiling reassuringly at her sister.

Lucilla regarded her dubiously. 'You seem different.'

'It's the brown hair,' Cara said. 'I look normal.'

'Cara, you're far too beautiful to ever look normal,' Lucilla murmured. 'No, it's something else. You seem really…worried.'

Drat. Her bathroom mirror had lied when it had reflected sophisticated confidence and she straightened her shoulders and blanked her mind of everything but where she was.

'It's this horrible competition. I hate being on show and the waiting is killing me.'

'I can imagine. It's a pity Aidan couldn't make it tonight.'

'Yes.' Cara swallowed the lump in her throat at the mention of Aidan's name. She had yet to tell her sister that the whole Aidan Kelly thing had been a ruse and she wasn't about to do so right now.

It had taken at least five drops of special eyedrops and six mushy teabags to clear the redness and swelling from her eyes as it was and the only reason she hadn't put contacts in was because she hadn't wanted to aggravate them more than the nonstop crying had.

Which was going to stop, too. Her heart might feel shattered by Aidan Kelly's rejection, but that didn't mean that her life had to be, as well.

And one way to make sure that it wasn't was to win this annoying competition and keep busy.

So far she had cried for almost twenty-four hours straight and she knew if she started thinking about Aidan she would start crying again and she couldn't afford to do that.

Her reputation was riding on her holding it together tonight and it was past time she looked out for herself instead of waiting for someone—Aidan—to come along and do it for her.

It was time for Juliet to grow a backbone and not let the loss of Romeo destroy her life.

Which was easier said than done when she knew how Juliet must have felt. Knew that her heart would have felt like someone had driven a knife right through the centre of it, the pain completely debilitating.

Sucking in a deep breath before her thoughts took a downwards spiral Cara placed her hand over her stomach and drew her spine up tall. She was fine. Or at least she would be fine. One day.

'Aidan's really busy right now but I think he'll be flying in sometime next week. But why don't you go home, Cilla? You look tired.'

And maybe it would be easier to pretend that her life didn't feel like it was hanging over the edge of a cliff without her sister's observant eyes on her all night.

'What about you? You must be feeling jet-lagged yourself.'

Cara felt numb most of the time and between that and yesterday's tortured tears it seemed to stave off the jet lag. 'I'll be fine. Really. Harriet said I was a shoo-in.'

Lucilla hesitated. 'I should stay.'

'You're no good to me if you fall over with exhaustion. Go home. I'll text you.'

'Are you sure you don't need me? I could—'

Cara put her hand on her sister's arm. 'You've always been there for me and I'm not sure I've ever told you how much it meant to me as a child. But I'm fine. Really.' She smiled. 'Please… You look shattered.'

As shattered as Cara probably looked beneath her carefully applied makeup.

'It's Christos. I swear he's the most… I don't even know

how to describe him!' Lucilla blazed, a curious light entering her eyes.

Lucilla had mentioned the tension between her and Giatrakos, but she had never seen Lucilla react like this before, and although Cara's curiosity was well and truly piqued as to what was going on with her sister, she knew that now was not the time to pursue it.

Instead she leaned forward and kissed Lucilla's cheek. 'I'm a big girl now. Stop worrying.'

Lucilla heaved a sigh. 'Okay.'

Cara watched her exit the swanky room and then turned back to the glittering crowd still in attendance. Usually, if she found herself alone in a crowd like this she wanted to run and hide because she knew almost everyone here was waiting for her to do something outrageous, every one of them holding their breaths in case the wild child struck again.

Well, she didn't intend to tonight.

Tonight, she was showcasing not only herself but Jenny's pearls that Aidan had given her.

Before leaving the island Cara had approached Jenny with the idea of importing her pearls and setting them up on the world stage.

Jenny had been overwhelmed and Cara had told her they'd start small. That she would buy a few pieces and wear them herself and see how they were received. If tonight was anything to go by, Jenny was going to need to open a factory.

'Miss Chatsfield, you look radiant tonight.'

Oh, no. She smiled at the elegant white-haired patriarch of the Demarche Group and sucked in her stomach. This was showtime.

'Thank you, Monsieur Demarche. I hope you're having a great evening.'

'Most definitely. And may I say that you look very elegant, my dear.'

Cara stared down at her navy blue gown. It was the most conservative piece of clothing she owned and if she wasn't wearing Jenny's pearls to lift the garment she'd feel completely boring. 'Thank you so much. It's such a pleasure to be here. I really appreciate you giving me this opportunity tonight.'

'I have to say, after last week, I wasn't sure which way to play this. You're a beautiful girl, Miss Chatsfield, but that Vegas hoopla came as a shock. As was the news that you and Aidan Kelly were an item. Tell me, my dear, is it serious?' He gazed around at the nearby guests and frowned. 'I would have expected to see him here with you tonight.'

And was her winning the contract riding on that? Cara frowned. And more importantly, did she want to win it if it was?

She recalled the paparazzi outside the hotel screaming the same question at her when her limousine had pulled up at the main entrance. This time she'd had the benefit of security and a barricade so she'd effortlessly deflected those questions by pretending that she hadn't heard them.

Unfortunately the only thing between her and the regal Monsieur Demarche was thin air, so pretending she hadn't heard him was probably not going to go down very well. Nor would walking off, but that was exactly what she felt like doing.

'Oh, he's…' About to pretend that Aidan was busy and that everything was rosy between them, Cara stopped. The truth was that she and Aidan had never been a real couple. And telling half-truths to save her skin wasn't the way she wanted to live her life anymore. Nor was burying her head in the sand when things went wrong.

She had changed, she realised with a faint smile. And she no longer felt like she needed other people's approval to feel like a success.

Feeling as though she was short of breath she stared at the Demarche patriarch, who had raised his eyebrow at her delayed response. 'The truth is, Monsieur Demarche.' She cleared her throat. 'The truth is, I've decided I don't want to be part of your business unless you want me for me and not because of what I'm wearing, or how I look, or who I'm seeing.'

The older man shook his head. 'Are you telling me you're pulling out of the running?'

'Yes.' Cara felt a tremulous smile form on her lips. 'Yes, I am.'

'But what will everyone think?'

'I don't know and I don't really care.' Cara raised her chin. 'I'm going to open a shop. It's what I've always wanted to do and it's time to live my life for me.'

And if that meant without Aidan, then...then... Her throat tightened. She couldn't think about that now because she had other things to do. 'But I thank you for the opportunity and for considering me,' she said graciously. 'And as for Aidan Kelly...well, he's—'

'Late.' Aidan pulled up beside her and gazed down at her. 'I'm so sorry, sweetheart.'

Cara's heart thumped inside her chest as she stared at the dashing figure he made in a tuxedo and...*tie*?

'You're wearing a tie.'

He pulled at his shirt collar as if it was strangling him. 'The occasion called for it. Bryce. Nice to see you again.'

'Aidan.'

He curved his arm around her waist and all she wanted to do was lean against his broad shoulders. 'I have to say,

I applaud your taste in spokesmodels. You couldn't have chosen better. Do you need another drink, darling?'

Darling? Oh, no, this was like the paparazzi rescue all over again. He was here because he felt sorry for her.

'Aidan, please, can I talk to you for a minute?'

'Of course.'

Cara smiled at Monsieur Demarche.

'I think we all underestimated you, my dear. If you should change your mind, please let us know.'

'I...' Cara felt choked up. 'Thank you. I think that's the nicest thing anyone has ever said to me.'

'Good luck with the future. Aidan, we should catch up sometime.'

Aidan nodded and took hold of Cara's arms. 'Of course. Now if you'll excuse me, Bryce, I'd like to talk to Cara in private.'

Cara felt as if she was in a daze as Aidan led her down a corridor and tested two doors before opening one and finding an empty room. 'Mind telling me what that was all about?'

Cara stared at him and blinked. 'I'm not sure. I think I just turned down a really lucrative job because I want to open a shop.'

Aidan gave her a slow, knowing grin. 'Good for you.'

Yes, good for her but... Her palms felt sweaty and she steeled herself to confront him. 'Look, Aidan. I appreciate you coming here. But I don't need you to do this for me. I'm fine.'

'Then you're doing better than me.'

Feeling like her heart was already in her mouth, Cara paused at his flat tone. 'What do you mean?'

'After you left I felt awful. Nothing seemed right and I wanted you with me.'

'But I offered to go with you and you told me not to.'

'A mistake I won't make again.'

'Aidan, you're not making any sense.'

Aidan shook his head. 'The AFL board think that as well.'

'Oh, God. I forgot. Did you save the business? Did you beat Ellery?'

'I don't know. I left Ben in charge of negotiations. As far as I know they're still going on. I haven't checked my phone.'

'You haven't checked your phone? And why are you smiling all of a sudden.'

'Because you were right, Cara.'

Feeling her pulse race at the unexpectedly heated look in his eyes Cara stared at him. 'Right about what?'

'So many things, sweetheart.'

'Aidan, please don't call me that. I—'

He took her face between his hands and her resolve to try and remain detached along with it. 'You were right about the fact that I was too emotional over Ellery—'

'Aidan, that's perfectly understandable after what he did to your family, but—'

He kissed her and Cara was so shocked that when he finally raised his head all she could do was stare at him mutely. 'Stop interrupting me, woman.'

'Okay.'

'And you were right about the fact that when you fall in love, really in love, you want to be with that person all the time. For the rest of your life, in fact.'

Cara's heart fluttered inside her chest like a bird flexing its wings for the first time. 'Did I say that?'

'Yes. And I'm hoping that's the way you feel about me.'

'Why would you hope that?'

'Because I think you're wonderful and I love you and I want to spend the rest of my life with you.'

Cara swallowed. 'You...love me?' She almost couldn't voice the word it sounded so surreal to her ears. 'You think I'm wonderful?'

Aidan grinned. 'Completely.'

Cara shook her head, not sure she wasn't dreaming. Hope warred with her deep-seated uncertainty and she couldn't think straight. It didn't help that he was holding her around the waist but when she tried to step back he held her fast.

'Sorry, sweetheart, I'm not letting you close yourself off from me again. Tell me what's wrong.'

Cara felt tears sting the backs of her eyes. 'You say all that to me now, but what about when I don't think before I act? What about when I hijacked your car—?'

'Borrowed,' he corrected.

She looked at him. 'I'm too impulsive for you. My life isn't as well planned out as yours. My reputation—'

'Cara, it doesn't matter. What matters is that when I'm with you I'm happy. When I look at your face I want to kiss you. When I hear your voice I want to listen to you. What matters is that without you my life is grey. You're the colour I didn't think I had time for and if I have a choice I don't want to go back to that. I need you, Cara, and I want to make you happy.'

'Really? Oh, Aidan.' Finally, Cara threw her arms around his neck. 'I can't believe it. I love you so much.'

'Thank God.' Aidan crushed her lips beneath his and neither one came up for air for a long time.

When Aidan finally lifted his head he smoothed her hair back from her face. 'I love you, Cara, and I'm sorry I hurt you yesterday. I'm sorry I didn't see what was right in front of my face. I'm sorry it took nearly losing you to see what I needed to see.'

'It's fine, Aidan.' Cara kissed the corner of his mouth.

'I won't ever leave you again. But you do know you still owe me a thousand pounds for breaking my shoes.'

Aidan threw back his head and laughed. 'You'll have to marry me to get that, doll face.'

Cara grinned. 'I did really love those shoes....'

Aidan slipped his hand around to the nape of her neck and tilted her face up to his for another searing kiss. 'And I love you. For ever.'

Cara's lip trembled and a tear slipped over the edge of her lash. Aidan groaned and whipped out a tissue.

Cara smiled as she took it and finally she knew that if there was one man's love she could always count on, it was this man's.

* * * * *

If you enjoyed this book, look out for the next installment of THE CHATSFIELD: BILLIONAIRE'S SECRET by Chantelle Shaw. Coming next month.

#3261 HIS FORBIDDEN DIAMOND
by Susan Stephens

Diamond dynasty heir Tyr Skavanga returns home haunted by the terrors of war. But one person defies his defenses...the exotically beautiful and strictly off-limits Princess Jasmina of Kareshi. With both their reputations at stake, can they resist their undeniable connection?

#3262 THE ARGENTINIAN'S DEMAND
by Cathy Williams

When Emily Edison resigns, her gorgeous billionaire boss, Leandro Perez, won't let her off easily. She'll pay the price—two weeks in paradise at his side! With her family's future at risk, Emily faces the ultimate choice—duty...or desire?

#3263 TAMING THE NOTORIOUS SICILIAN
The Irresistible Sicilians
by Michelle Smart

Francesco never thought he'd see Hannah Chapman again—a woman so pure and untouched has no place in his world. But a newly determined Hannah has one thing left on her to-do list. And only one gorgeous Sicilian can help her!

#3264 THE ULTIMATE SEDUCTION
The 21st Century Gentleman's Club
by Dani Collins

Behind her mask at Q Virtus's exclusive ball, Tiffany Davis reveals her true self—a powerful businesswoman with a proposal for Ryzard Vrbancic. He rejects the deal, but her ruthless determination makes him eager to seduce from her the one thing she's not offering....

HPCNM0714RB

REQUEST YOUR
FREE BOOKS!

2 FREE NOVELS PLUS
2 FREE GIFTS!

YES! Please send me 2 FREE Harlequin Presents® novels and my 2 FREE gifts (gifts are worth about $10). After receiving them, if I don't wish to receive any more books, I can return the shipping statement marked "cancel." If I don't cancel, I will receive 6 brand-new novels every month and be billed just $4.30 per book in the U.S. or $4.99 per book in Canada. That's a saving of at least 14% off the cover price! It's quite a bargain! Shipping and handling is just 50¢ per book in the U.S. and 75¢ per book in Canada.* I understand that accepting the 2 free books and gifts places me under no obligation to buy anything. I can always return a shipment and cancel at any time. Even if I never buy another book, the two free books and gifts are mine to keep forever.

106/306 HDN FVRK

Name _____ (PLEASE PRINT) _____

Address _____ Apt. # _____

City _____ State/Prov. _____ Zip/Postal Code _____

Signature (if under 18, a parent or guardian must sign)

Mail to the **Harlequin® Reader Service:**
IN U.S.A.: P.O. Box 1867, Buffalo, NY 14240-1867
IN CANADA: P.O. Box 609, Fort Erie, Ontario L2A 5X3

**Are you a current subscriber to Harlequin Presents books
and want to receive the larger-print edition?
Call 1-800-873-8635 or visit www.ReaderService.com.**

* Terms and prices subject to change without notice. Prices do not include applicable taxes. Sales tax applicable in N.Y. Canadian residents will be charged applicable taxes. Offer not valid in Quebec. This offer is limited to one order per household. Not valid for current subscribers to Harlequin Presents books. All orders subject to credit approval. Credit or debit balances in a customer's account(s) may be offset by any other outstanding balance owed by or to the customer. Please allow 4 to 6 weeks for delivery. Offer available while quantities last.

Your Privacy—The Harlequin® Reader Service is committed to protecting your privacy. Our Privacy Policy is available online at www.ReaderService.com or upon request from the Harlequin Reader Service.

We make a portion of our mailing list available to reputable third parties that offer products we believe may interest you. If you prefer that we not exchange your name with third parties, or if you wish to clarify or modify your communication preferences, please visit us at www.ReaderService.com/consumerschoice or write to us at Harlequin Reader Service Preference Service, P.O. Box 9062, Buffalo, NY 14269. Include your complete name and address.

SPECIAL EXCERPT FROM

HARLEQUIN®

Presents

*Harlequin Presents welcomes you to the
world of **The Chatsfield;**
Synonymous with style, spectacle…and scandal!*

*Read on for an extract from Chantelle Shaw's glittering
new edition to this series: **BILLIONAIRE'S SECRET***

* * *

"NICOLO, WAKE UP."

He groaned again.

Desperate to rouse him, Sophie touched his shoulder. "Nicolo…" She let out a startled cry when he suddenly gripped her wrist and gave a forceful tug. Caught off-balance, she fell on top of him.

"What's going on?"

"Nicolo—it's me, Sophie."

"Sophie?" His deep voice was slurred.

"Sophie Ashdown—remember me? You've been dreaming…."

There was silence for a few moments. "I grew out of wet dreams a long time ago," he drawled finally. "This is no dream. You feel very real to me, Sophie."

To Sophie's shock he tightened his hold on her wrist and moved his other hand to the small of her back, pressing her down so that she was acutely conscious of his muscular body beneath her. Only the sheet and her nightdress separated them. Sophie could feel the hard sinews of his thighs. She caught her breath as she felt something else hard jab into her stomach. Nicolo was no longer caught up in a nightmare; he was awake, alert—and aroused.

She hurriedly reminded herself that it was a common phenomenon for males to wake up with an erection, and it did not mean that Nicolo was responding to her in a sexual way. The same could not be said for her body, however.

"For goodness' sake, let me up," she said sharply, frantically trying to ignore the throb of desire that centered between her legs. To Sophie's horror she felt a tingling sensation in her nipples and prayed that Nicolo could not feel their betraying hard points through the sheet.

The pale gleam from the moon highlighted the hard angles of his face and the cynical curve of his mouth. Trapped against him, Sophie breathed in the spicy tang of his aftershave. It was a bold, intensely masculine fragrance that evoked an ache of longing in the pit of her stomach. Nicolo was the sexiest man she had ever met, and she was shocked by her reaction to his potent masculinity. "You were having a nightmare," she insisted. "I was trying to wake you. What other possible reason would I have for coming to your room in the middle of the night?"

* * *

*Step into the gilded world of **The Chatsfield!***
Where secrets and scandal lurk behind every door…
Reserve your room!
August 2014

HPEXP0714-2

Revenge and seduction intertwine…

Harlequin Presents welcomes you to the
world of The Chatsfield:
Synonymous with style, spectacle…and scandal!

Step into the gilded world of The Chatsfield!
Where secrets and scandal lurk behind
every door…

Reserve your room!